Invisible Magic

Also by Elisabeth Beresford

Dangerous Magic

Elisabeth Beresford

Invisible Magic

Illustrated by Reg Gray

DRAGON
GRANADA PUBLISHING
London Toronto Sydney New York

Published by Granada Publishing Limited
in Dragon Books 1978

ISBN 0 583 30267 X

First published in 1974 by Rupert Hart-Davis Ltd
Copyright © Elisabeth Beresford 1974

Granada Publishing Limited
Frogmore, St Albans, Herts AL2 2NF
and
3 Upper James Street, London W1R 4BP
1221 Avenue of the Americas, New York, NY 10020, USA
117 York Street, Sydney, NSW 2000, Australia
100 Skyway Avenue, Toronto, Ontario, Canada M9W 3A6
Trio City, Coventry Street, Johannesburg 2001, South Africa
CML Centre, Queen and Wyndham, Auckland 1, New Zealand

Made and printed in Great Britain by
Richard Clay (The Chaucer Press) Ltd
Bungay Suffolk
Set in Linotype Baskerville

TO
ALL THE CHILDREN OF
SPENCER PARK

Contents

1. *Elfrida*

If there was one thing that Roy Hatch really hated
it was people saying, 'Hallo, Roy! My word how

you've grown up. At least I think you have ...'

And then the person would look at him again in a puzzled sort of way and would probably pat Roy on the head before muttering something about being 'very busy; see you soon' and away the person would go.

Because the truth of the matter was that Roy hadn't grown more than 6·74 of an inch for three years. *He* knew exactly how much he had grown because he was measured at the beginning and the end of every term at Queensam Comprehensive School, just like everybody else was. The only difference being that everybody else shot up and up and up like runner beans in a good summer while Roy didn't.

It was all rather worrying and Roy saved up a lot of his pocket money and some of the money which he earned from doing a paper round and he bought a postal order and sent off for a book which was supposed to teach you exercises that would make you grow. Roy did everything the writer of the book suggested, but he didn't add more than a very small fraction to his height although he did seem to get a bit stronger, so that even if he was still the smallest boy in the P.E. class he was also the fastest at climbing up the ropes.

Which was something to be proud of and it did at least stop other boys (and girls come to that) getting too cheeky and calling him Midget or Half-Pint or Shorty all the time. But why grown-up people should keep telling him he'd grown, when he hadn't, was both mysterious and extremely annoying. So annoying in fact, that when Mr Forster of Oak Drive said it for the third time in one week as Roy arrived with the morning paper, Roy felt exactly like a kettle coming to the boil.

'I haven't grown,' said Roy, in a voice which was not unlike the rising shriek of a kettle, 'I haven't got taller by a quarter, or an eighth, or a twelfth.'

'Good, ah, yes,' said Mr Forster shaking out his paper and looking at it and then nodding his bald head, 'dear me, dear me. What *is* the world coming to? *I* don't know. 'Morning.'

'Or a sixteenth of an inch,' said Roy, coming off the boil slightly as Mr Forster vanished inside his neat little house. Losing your temper at about 7.00 in the morning can be an upsetting thing to do, and as Roy had now finished his paper round, he suddenly decided to ride his bicycle straight across the middle of Queensam Keep Park. It wasn't really a Park at all, but just a large squarish piece of dull grass in the middle of Queensam New Town and there were notices dotted all round it saying things like, 'No dogs', 'No bicycles', 'Do not leave Litter', 'Football and Cricket Forbidden'. With the result that most of the people who lived in Queensam never went near Keep Park in case they got into trouble for one reason or another. In fact, it had now got the nickname of 'Keep Off Park'. So for Roy to actually ride across it was really quite extraordinary, but then he was still in a temper and as it was early in the morning and going to be a very hot day, Keep Park was decidedly misty.

Roy looked left and right, but there wasn't anybody about except the milkman Mr Wickens at the very far end of Oak Drive, so Roy stood on his pedals and with a very satisfying thump his bike jolted over the pavement and on to the smooth grass and within seconds the white heat haze had made the rest of Queensam New Town quite invisible.

It was a funny feeling cycling into a sort of white emptiness, rather like exploring a cloud and Roy stopped feeling cross and began to enjoy himself as he swerved first one way and then another so that his newspaper sack flew out sideways. He got up a bit of speed and put one foot on the saddle and then he managed to edge his left foot on to the saddle too and finally he achieved what he called his 'flying eagle act' which meant hanging on to the handlebars, while his right foot was still perched on the saddle and his left foot was stuck up towards the sky. It was an act that needed speed (otherwise the bike developed a decided wobble), nerve and, most important of all no other traffic, people, buildings or animals anywhere near-by otherwise there would have been an accident.

'Zoom, Zoom, Zoom,' shouted Roy. 'Zoom, Zoom ... ooooooooooh.'

One moment there he was, almost in the middle of Keep Park with, as he very well knew, nothing and nobody within a hundred yards of his bicycle, and the next second his front wheel hit something extremely solid, the whole bike shuddered and Roy found himself going head over heels until he hit the ground with a crash that drove the breath out of him. It was like being tackled on the football field and for several seconds Roy thought that perhaps he had been winded in a third eleven match and had probably been hit on the head; at the same time he quite distinctly heard an irritated voice say,

'NOW look at what you'se done.'

'Not *you'se*,' Roy heard himself say, 'that's not grammar you know. You should say, "you have done". Oh help! I feel sick.'

'You'se, you've, thou hast,' muttered the voice, '*I* don't care. I don't care if you *are* sick either, so THERE. You've gone and been and done it and I'm out and *now* what happens?'

'*I* don't know,' said Roy, putting his head in his hands and rocking backwards and forwards. 'I feel awful, and who are you and what are you doing in the middle of Keep Park anyway?'

'What does anybody do in the middle of a Keep? I'm a prisoner of course! At least I was until you set me free. FREE! I'M FREE!'

'Don't shout,' said Roy, whose head was aching and he opened his eyes and looked around. There wasn't much to see, just his bike with the handlebars twisted at a nasty angle and the morning mist which was rapidly getting thinner and thinner as the sunlight grew stronger. There was no sign at all of anything solid enough to have caused a crash, let alone another person.

Roy took a deep breath, and got to his knees and

turned round very slowly, but there was absolutely nobody and nothing within a hundred yards of him, and for a moment, in spite of the warm sunshine the soles of his feet and the palms of his hands went cold and clammy.

'I've got concussion,' Roy said, 'that's what it is. Like the time I got pushed into the swimming bath and hit my head on the side. At least that's what they said I did, because I don't remember. You don't remember when you've had concussion. Your mind goes all blank and empty and...'

'You are *strange*! Do you always talk to yourself?' enquired the voice. It sounded as though it was about six inches away from Roy's right ear and as he knew perfectly well that there was nobody there, his own mouth stayed open for at least thirty seconds and then with a speed that would have astonished his P.E. teacher, Roy was on his feet, had seized hold of the bicycle, leapt on to the saddle and was stamping on the pedals. The bike was rather twisted and the brake pad made a complaining sound against the back wheel, but all Roy wanted to do was to get home as fast as possible.

'Oi, hey, watch it, LOOK OUT!'

The voice shouted rather breathlessly. It sounded so urgent that Roy actually slowed down, and it was just as well that he did for once again his front wheel hit an invisible something, there was a nasty screeching sound and the handlebars were twisted out of Roy's hands and he and the bicycle very slowly keeled over to the left until the pair of them fell in a tangle of legs, arms, pedals and spokes on to the grass.

'I did,' the voice said, puffing between every few words as it grew closer, 'I did try and warn you. Couldn't you see that there was a gap in the wall just to your left? No I suppose you couldn't. Are you all right?'

'No,' said Roy very loudly, 'I'm not at *all* right. In fact I'm probably quite ill. When I had measles and my temperature went up to 103 I could hear the television set in the house next door quite clearly. I suppose I've got a temperature now.'

There was quite a long silence during which Roy distinctly heard the thump-thump of his own heart, the tick-tock of his watch, the whirr-ssshhh of the still turning wheel of his bike, and the 'rummmm-rummmmm-rummmmm' of the traffic on the Motor-way. And then he heard something quite different. A most enormous sigh which was followed by a small 'Ooooooohhh. That's that then.'

It was said in such a sad way that Roy forgot to be scared for a moment.

'What's what?' he asked.

'Me being rescued.'

'Hang on, just let me think for a bit. How—how can a voice be rescued?'

'I'm not just a voice. I'm ME.'

'Who is me?' asked Roy, who by now was quite certain that not only had he got concussion and possibly sunstroke, but that he had also gone quite barmy as well.

'Princess Elfrida of the Castle,' the voice replied proudly, 'and anyway who are *you?*'

'Roy Hatch of Hatch Corner Stores.'

'Corner Stores?' said Elfrida. 'Um, would that be where you store things?'

'We store things for a bit and then we sell them, but look here.'

'Sell? Oh you mean *barter.* Exchanging one lot of things for another. That's a bike-cycle, isn't it?'

'No, not exactly, it's a bicycle. But look here...'

'I've always wanted to ride a bi-cycle' said the voice of Elfrida pronouncing the word very carefully. 'Can I have a go? It's quite simple, isn't it?'

'No it isn't and no you can't,' replied Roy. 'Now look here...'

But he spoke far too late for already his twisted, battered and dented bicycle suddenly began to heave itself upright. It was such an extraordinary sight that Roy, in spite of all that had happened in the last few extra-extraordinary minutes, couldn't quite believe it. And when he *did* believe the evidence of his own eyes, he was just that little bit too slow at making a grab for the rear mudguard as it swished past his face.

'OI, come BACK,' shouted Roy in his turn as his bicycle began to swerve first to the left and then to the right across Keep Park and, limping painfully, he took off in pursuit.

However, he soon discovered that if you are chasing after a bicycle whose rider you can see, you can, to a certain extent, anticipate which way they will twist and turn next. But if a bicycle has got an invisible rider it's quite impossible to work out what is going to happen next, so that one moment Roy was racing off to the left and then the next moment the bicycle would swoop away to his right.

Because of the most unusual circumstances Roy quite forgot that nobody was allowed to walk, let alone ride a bike across Keep Park and that as it was now well after seven o'clock other people would be about. He had very nearly managed to grab hold of the handlebars as they flashed past him when there was a kind of roaring from the road.

'Oi, YOU! What do you think you're playing at?'

Roy jumped round and realised, far too late, that all the mist had now cleared away and that the milkman, Mr Wickens was standing on the pavement shaking his fist. As Mr Wickens was renowned for his bad temper and he and Roy had never been on the best of terms it was just Roy's luck that the milkman who was also a town Councillor should catch him trespassing.

'Come here Shorty!' shouted Mr Wickens. 'Come here this minute, I say. *I'm* not running on that grass because it's not allowed, but that won't stop me reporting you my lad. No, indeed it won't, so you'd better come over here nice and quietly or you'll be in even worse trouble I can promise you!'

'But...' said Roy and then stopped, because what could he possibly say which would make the slightest bit of sense? HE knew that against all the rules and regulations, he had ridden his bicycle across Keep

Park, had then hit an invisible object in the summer mist, had fallen off his bike and bashed his head so that he was now having this sort of feverish dream in which his bike was being ridden by Elfrida-of-the-Castle with himself, Roy Hatch, chasing after it. Only of course, the whole story was complete nonsense and Mr Wickens would never, ever, in a thousand years believe one word of it.

Only while all this was whizzing through Roy's mind and he and Mr Wickens were facing each other across some dozen yards of grass on a nice warm summer's morning, there was a 'shhhh' and Roy's bike drew up alongside him and the voice of Elfrida buzzed in his ear.

'Are you in difficulties, Roy-of-the-Corner-Stores?'

'Yes I jolly well am and it's all *your* fault.'

'Why are you jolly about it?'

'It's just a way of saying things. I'm not jolly at all and...'

'Jolly,' shouted Mr Wickens. 'You've no right to be jolly my lad, I can tell you.'

'I don't like him,' buzzed Elfrida. 'He's just like all the village chiefs who are always complaining about the duck pond being too full of weeds or the hedges not being cut back properly. Only he's even worse than them. In fact he's a bit like old ... never mind. Shall I charge at him?'

'Don't you stand there mouthing at me,' roared Mr Wickens, his face going a deep red with anger. 'I won't stand for it, do you hear? Come off that grass IMMEDIATELY or I'll get the policeman.'

'But...' said Roy.

'Yes I—I—I JOLLY WELL shall charge,' said Elfrida. 'A bike cycle, sorry bi-cycle, isn't as exciting as a pony but it is better than nothing. One—two—three...'

'Stop,' shouted Roy. 'Stop, stop, stop, both of you. I don't like having a temperature and I want to wake up NOW.'

'CHARGE...' yelled the voice of the invisible Elfrida and the next second Roy's bike wobbled past him, gathered speed and headed straight for Mr Wickens the milkman. Mr Wicken's face changed colour from red to a kind of blotchy purple and then the purple turned into a blotchy white and as the bicycle bore down on him, Mr Wickens threw up his hands, turned round and started to run in a curiously jerky sort of way along the pavement to where his milk-float was parked. He reached it a mere five yards ahead of the charging bicycle and a good twenty yards ahead of Roy, for Roy had now given up trying to run properly, because he knew very well that you can never run in an ordinary way in dreams, so he was using a kind of jumpy walk.

Mr Wickens did a running dive into the float, started up and drove off as fast as he could with the float making a high-pitched whining sound. He shook his fist once out of the window and then the float squealed round the corner of Oak Drive with all its bottles rattling, and vanished up Oak Avenue.

'There,' said the voice of Elfrida somewhat unsteadily, 'that's got rid of *him*! He wasn't very brave, was he? Well, what happens next? It's your turn to help *me* again, because I've just rescued *you!*'

'What happens next,' said Roy very loudly, 'is that my alarm clock goes off and I stop dreaming you and everything else and I wake up and get dressed and go off on my paper-round. Excuse ME!'

And Roy picked up his bike and began to wheel it rather crookedly across the last few yards of grass, but even as he reached the edge of the pavement there were soft, running footsteps behind him and the last remaining copy of the *Queensam Post* was jerked out of his newspaper satchel. It fluttered under his nose for a moment as if it was being held in the hand of someone who was very upset and then, even as Roy stared at it with his mouth opening slowly until it was a perfect 'O', the *Queensam Post* was rolled up tightly into the shape of a cylinder so that the headline which had read, 'VANDALS DAMAGE TOWN HALL' now only showed 'VAND' and underneath this 'TOWN' and the next second after that Roy was desperately trying to defend himself as the newspaper fairly whizzed round his head. Fighting an invisible opponent was even more impossible than chasing an invisible cyclist and Roy staggered backwards as the *Post* caught him full in the stomach. His bicycle went in one direction and he went in another and for the third time that morning he hit the ground with a painful thud.

The newspaper waggled under his nose and the voice of Elfrida said furiously,

'I AM NOT A DREAM. I'M A PERSON THE SAME AS YOU! ALL RIGHT?'

Roy took a deep breath, held it, shut his eyes and counted up to twelve and then breathed out and opened his eyes. The *Queensam Post* was still being held some six inches from his nose.

'ALL right,' said Roy huskily. 'But—but what *does* happen now?'

'Well for a start off,' said Elfrida, 'I'm dreadfully hungry. It must be because I've been locked up as a prisoner for so long I suppose, so I'd like something to eat, please.'

'But,' said Roy, 'I can't just take your home and tell my grandmother that I've brought an invisible Princess back for breakfast.'

'I don't see why not. She *should* feel extremely honoured. The King, my father you know, *always* takes in travellers of every kind, but if you're going to be difficult about it don't say anything. After all I AM invisible and I won't be any trouble.'

'Promise?' said Roy getting slowly and rather painfully to his feet.

'Promise,' said the voice of Elfrida. 'Oh *do* get a move on. I'm starving.'

'O.K.,' said Roy, 'I'm pretty hungry too. But remember now, no trouble.'

'Of course not,' said Elfrida. 'I'm never, ever, any trouble.' And as she spoke she crossed two invisible fingers behind her back and then politely replaced the now somewhat battered copy of the *Queensam Post* in Roy's newspaper satchel.

2. *The Unwilling Knight*

'You've been gone a long time,' said Mrs Hatch. 'Why bless me, what have you been and done to yourself? And your bike too! You've not been in an accident, have you?'

Mrs Hatch, who was Roy's grandmother, came bobbing round from the back of the shop counter and stared at him while Roy muttered the first excuse that came into his head.

'I fell off my bike.'

'I can see that! What was it a car? A motorbike? A dog running across the road?'

'It was, it was all my fault. I hit, I hit, hit,' said Roy, sounding like a disc that had got stuck, 'I hit a stone. I think.'

'Are you *sure* you're all right?' asked Granny Hatch, wrinkling up her forehead, and she moved closer to Roy and stared at him very hard with her head back. This was because she wore bi-focal spectacles and she could only see close up things clearly if she looked through the bottom part of her glasses. She was exactly the same height as Roy, but about twice as wide as he was so that she was almost square in shape. Long, long ago when she was young she had lived in Wales and her voice still went up and down in a Welsh sort of way when she got upset about anything. It was going up and down quite a bit at this particular moment.

'Quite all right,' said Roy, who could feel his face starting to go red, 'except for being hungry.' And then, in spite of having had such an upsetting start to the day, he had a kind of brainwave and added, 'I think that having a bit of an accident can make a person twice as hungry as usual.'

'In-deed?' said Granny Hatch. 'Well there can't be much wrong with you if that's how things are. Off and wash those hands and your neck could use a flannel too, although I doubt that it'll get it. And for goodness sake boy, brush your hair. I don't wonder you ride into things, the way you've got your hair all over your eyes. Look like an old English sheepdog you do, and breakfast is all ready in the warmer and you can make more toast if you want it and...'

But Roy was already halfway down the passage, because he knew from past experience that once his Granny started talking it was almost impossible to get her to stop. The only thing to do was to walk away from her and she didn't seem to mind this treatment or to consider it rude, Roy spent quite a lot of his time at home with his Granny's voice lilting after him like the comfortable, familiar sound of gentle running water.

Roy had given Elfrida the most stern instructions as to how she was to behave and he had deposited her, at least her voice, which was all there was of her, in the narrow back alley at the rear of the Corner Stores. Roy scrabbled his way past the cardboard boxes of detergent and soap powders, and scrubbing powders and washing-up liquids, which always made the back of the Corner Stores smell so strongly of sheer cleanness that Roy often couldn't smell anything else for quite a long time after he'd got into the open air. Then there was the cold store, which even on the hottest day never lost its chilly atmosphere and finally there was a very small back yard with some dustbins in it and the door which led out into the alley. This was always kept locked, but it

never bothered Roy who neatly climbed up on to
the nearest bin, hauled himself up on to the wall,
carefully avoiding the bits of broken glass which
were arranged along the top of the wall and were
supposed to stop anybody climbing either in or out,
and looked up and down the alley. Not surprisingly
it looked as if it was quite empty.

'Oi,' said Roy softly. 'Oi, I say Elfrida.'

A ginger cat came padding out of the back yard of
the house next door and blinked yellow eyes at Roy.
Then it sat down and began to wash carefully
behind its ears.

'Oi,' said Roy a bit louder.

It was not a comfortable wall on which to balance
and he was starting to realise that what he'd told his
Granny was perfectly true. He was extremely hungry.

There was no answer and Roy had just begun to
say angrily, 'Oh well that's that then. And good
riddance too...' when the cat sat bolt upright and
stared very hard at something with the very end of its
tail twitching. Then it got to its feet and slowly, head
stretched forward, sniffed at something. Its head went
down a little in a series of small jerks and its back
rose up and faintly at first and then with increasing
pleasure it began to purr.

There could be no doubt about it, the ginger cat
was being tickled behind the ear by an invisible
hand.

'Elfrida,' said Roy furiously, 'stop that and come
here. I'm getting cramp. Why didn't you answer
me when I called?'

'Sorry,' said Elfrida and she appeared to have stopped stroking as the cat was patting hopefully at the empty air with one paw while its back was sinking into a straight line. 'Sorry, only I think I must have gone to sleep for a moment ... I feel almost as sleepy as I do hungry ... ooooooooh.'

'Oh do come on,' snapped Roy, 'or Granny'll be looking for me. If you put one foot on the handle and the other on that brick that sticks out it's quite easy to get up here.'

'But I can't climb in this dress,' said Elfrida. 'It's my best one. It's got GOLD stitching.'

'I don't care if it's got a diamond zip, if you want to have any breakfast you've jolly well got to climb over this wall. *I* don't want you to, I don't care *what* you do. So if you want to go on being silly about your dress you can jolly well stay where you are. Good-bye.'

'No, No I'm coming. Oh I hate you,' said Elfrida whose temper was rapidly becoming as bad as Roy's. Anyway the cat put back its ears and went streaking off down the alley and vanished in the hot, hazy sunlight. There was some muttering and a creaking sound and then Elfrida said in a voice which had become as chilly as the Cold Store in December, 'If you would be so kind as to hold out your hand I will do my best to climb this horrid wall.'

Roy edged further forward on his stomach and stretched his hand down as far as he could and then for a second he was in danger of loosing his balance altogether, for out of thin air he felt, even if he couldn't see it, Elfrida's small, warm hand clutch his and suddenly she stopped being a dream or an impossibility and became a person.

'Heave,' said Roy and tugged and Elfrida hung like a dead weight for a moment and then she must have found the brick on which to perch and Roy nearly went backwards with a rush that would have taken him right over the dustbins.

There was a faint tearing sound and a gasp from Elfrida, and then she only too obviously *did* lose her balance and there was a crash as a dustbin lid went flying. Roy felt wildly round for Elfrida's hand, found it and dragged her protesting, hobbling and gasping into the passage and helter skelter past all the packing cases and somehow managed to push her into the kitchen just as his Granny appeared in the back doorway of the shop.

'What ARE you doing, boy?' she demanded. 'You haven't washed, in fact you're even more dirty than you were before. Where you find all the dirt I *don't* know. Queensam's supposed to be such a clean sort of a place, but then you'd find mud and dust and goodness knows what in a raft in the middle of the Atlantic Ocean I daresay. Now will you go and WASH . . .'

'Yes, Gran. O.K., Gran.'

'And have your breakfast before its dried to nothing. Oh I'm coming, I'm coming . . .' This last remark was addressed to a customer who was now calling from the front of the shop. 'I can't be in two places at once now can I? Although I do my best I'm sure. Well then, what can I help you with, Mrs Swift? . . .'

Roy shut the kitchen door, leant against it and let out a faint sigh of relief before going over to the table and putting another bowl on it.

'Sit down,' he said, 'and have some cornflakes. We're safe for a bit, because that Mrs Swift talks even more than Granny so even if she's only come in to buy a duster, she'll stay for ages. Sometimes she stays here all the morning.'

'It doesn't look like corn,' said Elfrida. 'At least not like the corn *we* grow. I mean, of course, the *farmers* grow . . . that is.'

She sounded rather embarrassed, but Roy was too busy eating to pay much attention to her and it wasn't until he had nearly finished his own cornflakes that he glanced up and was greeted by the sight of a spoon becoming invisible as it entered Elfrida's mouth. His own spoon stayed suspended in mid-air as he watched first the tip, then half, then the whole of the rounded part of the spoon vanish, only to reappear completely a few seconds later.

'It's rude to stare,' said Elfrida reprovingly. 'It's not at all like our corn, and it's far too sweet, but it's not bad in a squashy sort of way. What's next?'

'What?' said Roy, who was now staring at the spoon going round and round the plate, for far too sweet or not it was obvious Elfrida wasn't going to waste a scrap.

'What—is—next—please?'

'Oh, hang on, I'll see.'

It was Marmite, fried bread and scrambled eggs which Roy divided with scrupulous fairness into two helpings, and when *that* was all gone—which it did at surprising speed—he made four slices of toast, and although Elfrida wouldn't have any home-made strawberry jam, as again she said it was too sweet after one small taste, she made very short work of the remains of the Marmite pot and half a pint of milk.

'Do you always eat such a lot?' asked Roy, his spirits sinking because he was dimly starting to realise that if Elfrida was going to be around the Corner Stores for long she'd get through a remarkable amount of food. (Now he understood what his Granny meant when she said she'd rather 'keep him for a week than a fortnight'.)

'Oh no,' Elfrida replied, smothering a gigantic yawn. 'But then you know I haven't eaten properly for ages and ages.'

'Nor have I. Not since supper last night.'

'Silly, I *mean* ages and ages. What's the date today?'

'It's about August the twenty-second. Or it could be the twenty-third.'

'NO! I mean the YEAR.'

Roy told her and Elfrida gave a kind of gasp and then there was a long silence during which Roy could hear his Granny and Mrs Swift both talking at the same time in the shop.

'As long as *that*,' whispered Elfrida. 'Why, I've been a prisoner for hundreds and hundreds of years.

Oh dear, oh dear. OH DEAR.' And there was a loud sniff.

'You're not going to cry are you?' Roy asked in alarm.

'No, of course I'm not,' said Elfrida, her voice getting higher and higher. 'Only it's not very nice you know, waking up to find that you're hundreds of years old and invisible as well ... oooooh.'

'Here hang on,' said Roy. 'I've got a handkerchief somewhere, no I haven't ... yes, I have, it's a bit dirty, but it's only off my bike so it's clean dirt. Go on, blow.'

The crumpled handkerchief wavered across the kitchen table and Elfrida did as she was told and then handed it back again. It seemed to have stopped her crying, but her voice was still very husky as she said,

'Well I bet you jolly well wouldn't like it, if it happened to you.'

'No, no probably not,' agreed Roy. 'Look here there's a lot we've got to get straightened out, at least I have. About what's going to happen to you and everything, but we can't talk here. There's a tank room—well it's more like an attic really but it'll have to do—over *my* room. We'd better get you up there for safety.'

'You want to make me a prisoner again don't you?' Elfrida demanded and her chair scraped backwards across the vinyl flooring as though she'd got up suddenly in alarm.

'No of course I don't. Don't be stupid. I'm thinking

about you're being *safe*. There's no lock and key or bolts or anything on the door, so I couldn't make you a prisoner if I wanted to. I'll show you in a tick if...'

'What's a tick?' Elfrida spoke from near the doorway which showed how nervous she was, because she must have tip-toed round the table to get there.

'A tick's like a few seconds or a minute. Or how long you want it to be really. I must do the washing up first though and you can help. Come on.'

Roy was already learning that the only way to stop Elfrida being silly or taking fright, or even just going to sleep, was to tell her to do something very firmly.

Roy washed and Elfrida dried and once Roy had got over a nervous twitch about making a grab for a cup or a plate as it floated off the draining board, they got through everything in a matter of minutes.

'Granny,' said Roy putting his head round the door and into the shop where Mrs Swift was leaning against the counter on her side and talking nineteen to the dozen while Mrs Hatch leaned on her side and talked too,

'Gran, I'm just going up to the loft to put out my train set. O.K.?'

'Still playing with trains,' said Mrs Swift. 'A big boy like you! You seem to grow every time I see you.'

Roy gave her the sort of smile he kept for one particular master at school and the Alsatian at No. 10 Oak Crescent, and then stepped backwards before his Grandmother could manage to say anything. He pushed Elfrida up the stairs and her dress must have had a very long skirt, because he stood on it twice and on the second occasion they had a whispered and furious argument, and it wasn't until Roy had actually managed to get her into the attic and had shown her the boltless trapdoor and the skylight window which she could open from the inside, that she quietened down a bit.

'Flip,' said Roy, unrolling the sleeping bag which he'd brought up from his own room and then sitting down on it heavily. 'And I thought these holidays were going to be dull, like holidays always are.'

'What does flip mean?' asked Elfrida from the direction of the skylight.

'I don't know and I don't care. Now *please* try and pay attention because I'm going to ask you some questions. First...'

'I'd never realised how flat everything is,' said Elfrida, her invisible breath misting up the skylight glass, 'when it's all covered in forests everything seems to roll up and down a bit. From my turret it always made me think of a coverlet lying on top of a bed that hadn't been well made. What a lot of castles there are now. You've got castles everywhere!'

'First, how long are you going to stay ... What do you mean castles everywhere?' asked Roy getting to his feet and joining Elfrida at the window. 'There aren't any castles in Queensam. At least not that I've ever seen. It's a New Town you know.'

'Then what are those?'

'What are what?'

'Where I'm pointing of course. Oh bother. Oh

flip. Of course you can't see. Um, well to the left. There's an ENORMOUS castle over there.'

Roy wondered again for a fleeting second if he could be having a really very vivid dream and then a sharp finger digging into his left shoulder re-assured him that invisible or not, hundreds of years old or not, Elfrida was in her own way extremely real and he opened the window and peered as far to the left as he could. Shimmering in the heat of the August day rose the tall, white shape of Queen-sam Towers, Flats 1 to 80.

'That's not a castle,' said Roy. 'That's—that's a lot of houses one on top of each other.'

'There's no thatch,' Elfrida said suspiciously.

'They don't use thatch for houses any more, I think,' Roy added and he craned out even further because he wanted to make quite sure that the planners of Queensam New Town hadn't added a touch of thatch anywhere. But all he could see, apart from the Towers—which was the biggest block of all—was the usual group of smaller flats; the Council Chambers which somehow always made him think vaguely of a large ship; the blinding glitter of the sun on the hundreds of windows at the school; the criss-cross of medium-sized buildings which made up the shopping precinct, and then the lines and semi-circles of two and three storey buildings which, rather like the threads in a spider's web, were spun out from the centre of the New Town.

'No, there's no thatch and no castles,' said Roy and leant his chin on his folded hands and stared out towards Queensam Park. It was quite empty. Or was it? Just for a split second in the hazy heat which shimmered over the untrodden grass, could he see a kind of shadowy outline of four walls with bits sticking up at the corners?

Roy, who had excellent eyesight, blinked hard and looked again. No, there was nothing there. It had only been because he'd been looking directly towards the sun that his eyes had cheated him, because now he could see clear across the Park to the distant Motorway with its steady lines of cars, lorries, juggernauts and vans.

'Now then,' said Roy turning towards where he hoped Elfrida might be standing, 'as I was saying, I've got some questions to ask *you*. First of all how long are you going to stay here?'

'I don't know,' said Elfrida from the direction of the sleeping bag. 'What a funny sort of bed. Oh it undoes. Isn't that clever! I think I might sleep for a little while...' The sleeping bag moved up and down in bumps, the zip did itself up again and a definite hollow appeared in the pillow. The voice of Elfrida said,

'It's very tiring you know, being rescued after such a long time. I suppose I'll be staying here—and it's not at all what I'm used to, but it'll have to do—until you finish rescuing me.'

'What do you mean, *finish* rescuing you?' Roy demanded.

'Why, make me visible again of course,' replied Elfrida. 'After all, it's no good my being free if no one can see me, is it? Good night. Or perhaps I should say good morning.'

And the sleeping bag humped itself slightly and began to move slowly up and down as its invisible occupant went instantly and silently to sleep.

3. The Top of the Tower

It slowly became obvious that Elfrida, as well as being a champion eater, was very good at sleeping too as the humps and bumps in the sleeping bag hardly stirred when on three occasions Roy went and spoke quite loudly where he hoped Elfrida's ears might be. After the third go he gave it up, wisely deciding that, all things considered, a sleeping Elfrida was likely to be far less trouble than an awake and possibly hungry Elfrida. So Roy wrote out a message which he pinned on the loft side of the trapdoor. It said,

E. Stay here. Safer. Back soon. R.

Then it occurred to him that perhaps if she did wake up she might get bored and anyway she wouldn't understand how to use his train set for company as it was electric, so he nipped back to the shop to get her something to read.

'Something,' thought Roy, wrinkling up his fore-head in a ferocious scowl, 'something that'll bring her up to date if she really *is* hundreds of years old.'

But which out of all the newspapers, magazines, comics and paperback books that were sold at the Corner Stores, was the right one for somebody who was, to put it mildly, rather out of touch with current events? All the newspapers were so up to the minute all right with their news, but they didn't seem to write anything about what had happened last week, let alone a year ago, so they were no good. And he didn't really think that when it came to the maga-zines Elfrida would be interested in Boxing or Motor Cycle Racing or even Cricket as they probably hadn't even been invented as far as she was concerned. However, there were of course, the magazines espe-cially for ladies and Roy, going rather red around the jawline while squinting out of the corner of his

eye to make sure that his Granny was busy serving
ice-creams out of the deep freeze, had a quick look
at what was offered here. Would Elfrida be interested in how to knit a sweater, or how to make rock
cakes or how to take a vacuum cleaner to pieces?
Somehow it didn't seem likely.

Roy turned to the comics. They were even less use
because how could Elfrida possibly understand *The
Adventures of Jet-Star* or *Diggy-Doggy Super-Dog*?
And when he came to the paperback books it was
even worse because they all seemed to be about
detectives or spies or soldiers or animals or even
crossword puzzles. Until that is, Roy discovered a
somewhat tattered book which was called:

Queensam! What's On. Summer Holidays!

It looked pretty dull, but at least it was about the
neighbourhood and it had some pictures in it. Even
more important, it was free. So Roy slipped it out of
the rack and took it upstairs to where the sleeping
bag was going up and down and left it by where
he hoped Elfrida's nose might be.

'You're still looking peaky, boy,' said Granny
Hatch as Roy joined her behind the counter. 'Which
I can't understand considering the amount of breakfast you've eaten. I'd rather keep you a week than
a fortnight, so I would!'

Fortunately for Roy, Saturdays were always very
busy and his Granny didn't get a chance to ask him
any more questions, and they even had to have their
mid-day meals at different times because the lunch
hour was the busiest time of all. Then the Stores

was shut until 5 o'clock when the evening papers were due to come in to be sorted and delivered, so Granny, with a great sigh of relief, went upstairs to her room to take off her shoes and have a nap and Roy was about to go and call on Elfrida for the fourth time when he heard her say,

'Pssst,' from the bend of the stairs.

'Don't DO that!' whispered Roy, who had nearly fallen backwards out of sheer surprise.

'Sorry,' said Elfrida, not sounding it in the least, 'but it got a bit lonely up in your turret. I could hear everybody talking downstairs and I thought I'd come down and listen.'

'Well they've all gone now. Let's go out for a bit. I hate being indoors.'

'Not half as much as I do,' replied Elfrida. 'Just you wait until *you've* been indoors for a few hundred years and then see how much you like it!'

'I've been thinking,' said Roy, 'and the first thing I'm going to do is to borrow a dog.'

'?' said Elfrida.

'Because I'm going to look barmy if I seem to be talking to myself, but people never take any notice if you're speaking to a dog. I wish we had a dog, but there are so many "no dogs allowed" notices in this place that it's no fun for a dog living here. So I'll borrow Mr Cliff's from up the road. It's pretty old and wheezy, but it'll do.'

Mr Cliff's dog was called Bouncer, which was about the most unsuitable name it could have had, as it had lost any bounce it might once have had a long time ago. Mr Cliff and his dog looked rather alike with their white hair, white moustaches and sad brown eyes.

'Going to take him for a walk? Mind he doesn't run away with you. Haw, haw, haw,' said Mr Cliff as he handed over Bouncer's lead. 'Enjoy yourselves, though what you'll find to do in this dish-water place I CAN'T imagine. Oh well, back to work.'

Bouncer made Elfrida's acquaintance round the next corner and like the ginger cat didn't seem to mind her invisibility, he even put up one shabby paw to have it shaken.

'He's not much like our dogs,' said Elfrida. 'Ours are much, much, MUCH bigger because we use them for hunting in the forests. When did you chop down all the forests?'

'It wasn't me, I never chopped down anything. We're not allowed to chop down trees these days. Now then Elfrida, look here, just how are we supposed to make you visible?'

'It's quite simple. We'll just go and see your local magician.'

'We haven't got one,' said Roy stopping dead in the middle of a zebra crossing, much to the irritation of a large, red-faced man who was sitting in the back of a very grand, chauffeur-driven car.

'Get a move on,' said the chauffeur, leaning out of the window, and although he sounded quite fierce he grinned and jerked his head back a fraction and Roy saw that the fat man was Mr Williams, the Mayor, so he moved with great speed.

'Then who,' said Elfrida, catching up with him, 'who puts spells on you to make you better when you're ill? Your chariots smell nasty but they move very *fast* don't they?'

'The doctor does and he's not a magician, and yes they do, and they're not chariots, they're cars, and I don't *know* any magicians. There was a conjuror who came down for the Christmas show last year, but I don't think that's the same as a real magician.'

'Well then, who is your wisest old person?'

'My Granny,' replied Roy, 'but we're not asking her! She'd have a fit if she knew she'd got an invisible Princess living in the loft.'

'Well, what about a star-watcher or a dream-diviner or a reader-in-sand?'

'We haven't got any of *them*,' said Roy, who was beginning to feel that he was letting the twentieth century down pretty badly one way and another.

'A—keeper of illuminated manuscripts?' suggested Elfrida rather desperately.

'I don't know what that is.'

'Yes, you do. You gave me one. Here...'

And a very crumpled copy of *Queensam! What's On* suddenly materialised under Roy's nose.

'Is *that* an illuminated manuscript?'

'Yes, and a very bad one it is too, but it'll have to do. Who did the writing?'

There didn't appear to be any author's name, but at the bottom of the last page it said 'produced by Queensam Public Library' in rather smudgy small letters and as it was the only lead they had, Roy did a fast left turn and headed for Queensam Towers which housed the library on the ground floor. It was a ten minute walk during which Bouncer tried to stop at every tree and Elfrida kept harping on about how much better things used to be, until between the two of them Roy lost his temper just as they entered the echoing, deserted main hall.

'Now look here,' he said in a furious whisper. 'I didn't *ask* to rescue you! I didn't ask you to come home with me! I didn't want to come to the library because I'm going to look a perfect nit asking silly questions about magicians and spells and things. But I DID rescue you, although I don't know how, and I'm beginning to wish I hadn't, and I *did* take you home *and* I gave you a jolly good breakfast and somewhere safe to sleep and I AM trying to help. So jolly well shut up about everything being so much better where you came from. And anyway...' added Roy, working himself up even further as he considered the injustice of the situation, 'if everything was so marvellous *why* did you get locked up in the first place?'

Roy's voice had risen quite a lot by the end of this as it's very difficult to be furious in a whisper and as he said the word 'place' three things happened more or less at once.

Elfrida stamped her foot hard on the marble-type floor and shouted,

'Don't you *dare* to talk to me like that!'

A man's voice, and an unpleasantly familiar one at that, said from somewhere inside the library,

'Who's making that infernal din out there?' and there was the slap, slap of hurried footsteps. At the same moment someone in the flats pushed the bell for the lift and the doors began to squeak shut. Bouncer, who was lying spread-eagled on the cool floor, wheezing and rolling his eyes, quivered to his feet and, under the mistaken notion that the squeaky door was some kind of interesting rat, skittered off towards it at a surprising speed in one of his age, taking Roy with him as Roy had Bouncer's lead wrapped round his wrist. Bouncer might be old, but he was still a medium-sized dog and Roy was not a very large boy and furthermore he had been caught completely off balance so that one second he was arguing with Elfrida and the next he found himself being pulled through the narrowing gap of the closing lift door.

'Stop!' shouted Elfrida.

'Stop at once!' called the unpleasantly familiar voice and Mr Wickens the milkman came hurrying out of the library and for the second time that day caught Roy doing something which was forbidden in Queensam. For neither Roy nor Elfrida had noticed that there were two large notices just outside the block which said,

'NO DOGS ADMITTED' and 'SILENCE'.

Mr Wickens thudded across the entrance hall with his hand outstretched towards the lift button, because he was quite determined to stop Roy getting away from him this time. Bouncer made excited little snorting sounds and tried to get out, while Roy tried

to hold him back and he shouted despairingly,
  'Elfrida! Elfrida!'

A tall, pale faced young man with long hair and a
beard and with very thick spectacles came hurrying
out of the library with his arm full of books and said

'Please, please can we have a little less noise. Oh
it's *you* Councillor Wickens, I'm sorry. At least,
even if it is *you* please could you be quieter?'

'Got you,' said Mr Wickens, paying no attention
at all to the young man, and he made a pounce for
the lift button and then the smile of triumph
vanished from his face and he pulled his hand back
as though it had been stung.

'Wow! What! Where? Who?' said Roy as Elfrida
pushed through the long-suffering sliding doors
which at last squealed together with a click.

'It's me,' said Elfrida somewhat breathlessly. 'Did
you see his face? I jabbed his hand with one of my
pins. It was the nasty man I rescued you from this
morning, wasn't it? So now we're equal again as
I've rescued *you* twice! Is he always cross like that?'

'Most of the time. Granny says he could curdle a
bottle of milk just by looking at it. Thanks for the
rescue and I'm sorry about what I said just now,
but...'

'But, I know,' agreed Elfrida, indistinctly as she was
about to put the pin back in her hair so that at this
particular moment she was holding it between her
teeth. 'Being worried about things always makes
you more cross than worried somehow. I say, are
we flying like a dragon?'

'No, we're going up in a lift. It's instead of having to climb stairs.'

Elfrida was about to say, 'you don't have to use your legs much, do you ...' as she was thinking about Roy's bicycle and the car-chariots and now this latest flying-lift, which was starting to make her feel a bit sick in her invisible stomach, but she didn't want Roy to start getting angry again, so for once in her life she wisely held her tongue.

The lift hissed to the second floor, but whoever had rung for it had got tired of waiting and when the doors squealed open there was nobody there, although the cross, complaining voice of Mr Wickens could still be heard quite easily saying,

'... shall put in a strong complaint! *And* I intend to bring the subject up at the Council Meeting this evening ...'

Roy hastily pushed the button for the top floor and the lift resumed its smooth journey upwards with Elfrida pressing her lips more and more firmly together. However, when they finally reached the 21st storey the view was worth a bit of travel-sickness.

Roy had never been up to the top of the Towers before and he forgot all his troubles as he gazed out of the window. The heat of the day made everything shimmer and shake and the horizon was lost in a soft blue haze which might possibly be the English Channel. He could definitely see towns and villages, an airfield, miles and miles of hopfields with their regular criss-cross lines, a long stretch of the Motorway where the traffic seemed to be moving at half speed because it was some distance away, a great many church steeples all of which appeared to be surrounded with a shawl of trees and, closer at hand, there was Queensam itself looking, from this height, like a neat toy town.

'There's the Corner Stores,' said Roy, 'and Mr Cliff's house and Oak Crescent and my School, and there's Woolworth's and Boots and the car park for the Hospital and I *think* that's old Wickens...'

The window wasn't made to open so Roy had to press his forehead right up against the glass to look down at what appeared to be a head with two feet with no body in between. Another head, this time with long yellow hair, came running up and apparently tried to speak to Mr Wickens and was waved away by a hand. The yellow head shook itself in a sad way and retreated into the Tower block, while Mr Wickens squeezed himself into what looked like a matchbox-sized car and drove off in the direction of the Town Hall.

'Thank goodness,' said Roy, 'now it'll be safe to go down again. Ouch, don't *do* that!'

'Sorry,' said Elfrida, who had suddenly grabbed Roy's arm, 'but look down there, over to the right.'

'That's Keep Park. Where you were ... oh!'

From the 21st storey they had a very good view indeed of that dull stretch of grass, only from this height it was just a little more interesting for quite clearly, criss-crossing this way and that, were some very definite bicycle tracks. They were like two triangles joined together to make a kind of six-pointed star and, in the middle of the star, was an oblong shape with a bulge at each corner.

'Oh dear,' said Roy swallowing, 'I didn't realise how much it would show up, but perhaps nobody'll see it at ground level. Although if you look very hard from up here you can see other marks as well. Footpaths and a circle and a few lines. Perhaps it's the way the grass gets cut.'

'No it isn't,' said Elfrida in such a strange voice that it made Roy get a shiver down his back. 'I don't know what that *big* long shape is over by the road, but I know that little path over to the right. It leads from the kitchen to the well where we get our water and that funny shaped bit on the other side of the well is where I found a whole lot of ever so pretty shiny bricks with patterns on them. Rather like those bricks you've got in your kitchen.'

'Shiny...? Oh you mean tiles I suppose, but Elfrida...'

'Don't you see,' said Elfrida, who was obviously hopping from foot to foot with excitement, 'the shape of everything is still *there*. And you being able to see it too makes me feel not quite so invisible. Let's go lowering at once.'

'Go?'

'Lowering. If it's a lift coming UP, it must be a lower going DOWN. Oh do come up.'

And Elfrida picked up Bouncer who had gone fast asleep in his usual star-fished position and hurried over to the lift and pushed the button, saying over her shoulder, 'Now if we can find the man who did the writing of the manuscript and tell him what we've seen, he's sure to know what to do to make everything all right.'

'You'd better let me do the talking,' said Roy as they reached the ground floor, but Elfrida was far too excited to listen to this excellent advice and she ran out of the lift and was halfway across the echoing entrance hall before Roy could stop her. The young librarian who had been standing miserably by the main door on the instructions of Mr Wickens, turned round and said,

'I say. Excuse me, but dogs aren't allowed in here and Councillor, Councillor...' And the young man's voice suddenly went right down into a deep bass note as he quite distinctly heard someone say.

'Oh, are you the writer of illuminated manuscripts? Please, please will you help me?'

The words might be a little unusual, but it wasn't that which turned the young man's normally pale face as white as the pile of papers he was holding. It was the fact that the words appeared to be spoken by a medium-sized, very old dog who was without doubt jogging across the ground floor of the Tower Block a good three feet *off the ground*.

'Elfrida...' Roy shouted. 'Don't...'

But it was too late, for the young man was already slowly sinking to the ground as his knees buckled under him, his eyes rolled upwards and his papers went 'swish-swish-swish' in all directions.

'Oh—oh—oh FLIP!' said Elfrida-of-the-Castle.

4. *The First Spell*

The young man opened his eyes reluctantly and shook his head.

'No, no take it away, nasty smell,' he said.

'I told you it wouldn't work—burning a feather under his nose,' said a voice.

'But it *has* worked,' said a second voice triumphantly. 'Wasn't it lucky that I had a swan's feather with me? They use them for stuffing pillows you know. I mean *we* use them for pillows. Are you better now.'

'Not really,' said the young man, and he took off his spectacles with a very shaky hand and cleaned them on his tie and then put them on again. He *seemed* to be inside the library which was nice and reassuring, and there was a boy with a lot of dust on his forehead leaning over him and looking worried. It was a face he thought he recognised and after a few seconds careful thought he said,

'Queensam Comprehensive. Er—Thatch?'

'Hatch, Roy,' said the boy, and then he glanced over his shoulder and added, 'Do throw away that feather, it's a horrible stink.'

The young man followed the progress of a singed and smoking feather across the library with his eyes until the feather vanished inside a tin waste bin. Then he shook his head and said carefully,

'My name, is Hugh. Hugh Patrick. How do you do? I suppose I slipped and banged my head. I must have banged it pretty hard because I seem to keep hearing voices and seeing quite impossible things...'

'I'm not an impossible thing, I'm just invisible. That's all...'

'Shhhhhh.'

'No I'm not going to shhhh. I think he's got a very

nice face, its not red or cross like most of the faces in your town, and because he's got a nice face I'm going to ask him to help me.'

'He'll think he's gone mad,' said Roy, making one last effort to keep the situation under control, 'and he's not a manuscript-illumer-what-name. He's the Children's Librarian, it says so on his desk.'

'I don't care. You see Mr Hugh, my name's Elfrida and I've been locked up in a castle for hundreds of years until Roy set me free, quite by mistake actually, only I'm invisible. Please, do you think you can help me?'

'Dear me,' said Mr Patrick, settling himself more comfortably against the side of his desk and clasping his arms around his knees. 'Dear, dear me. It must be very awkward.'

'Do—do you believe her?' whispered Roy.

'I don't see why I shouldn't,' replied Mr Patrick. 'Of course I've never met an invisible young lady before. It's a most interesting experience.' And he added under his breath, 'It's the knock on my head of course. Or—it could be overwork...'

'Well that's all right then,' said Roy, feeling extremely surprised at this quite astonishing good sense being shown by a grown-up person. 'I suppose I'd better tell you what's happened so far.' And he began to talk very fast so as to stop Elfrida butting in too much and Mr Hugh Patrick nodded and said 'dear me' occasionally, and even made a few notes on the back of an old envelope.

It was a great relief to have an older man to talk

to and it was only the distant chiming of the Town Hall clock which made Roy realise how late it was. As Mr Patrick was quite convinced that he was now having a pleasant and most interesting day-dream as a result of his fall, he was soon only too anxious to help, even rashly promising to see if he could track down some useful magic books in the library, and as a stop-gap he pressed two of E. Nesbit's magic novels into Elfrida's invisible hands.

'I *told* you he'd help,' said Elfrida as they hurried back with poor old Bouncer panting along in the rear.

'Um,' replied Roy, 'it just seems a bit odd that he should that's all. Now look here Elfrida, while I'm off on my paper round please, please keep quiet in the loft.'

'Oh I will,' Elfrida promised. 'Now that I've got these illum... sorry, books to read that Mr Hugh gave me, I won't be bored at all. Only...' And she gave that deep sigh which Roy was learning to dread a little.

'Only, I'm getting EVER SO hungry,' said Elfrida and she sniffed loudly as they passed a café which had a notice outside.

'CHINESE FOOD TO TAKE AWAY.'

'Oh Glory,' said Roy and, handing Bouncer's lead to Elfrida, he went into the café and ordered a double portion of Pekin fish fingers and Canton sweet and sour chips. The sooner the Children's Librarian did something the better.

And it wasn't until some hours later when Roy

was on the very edge of being asleep that he realised
that although it had been a most worrying, anxious
and even expensive day, since he had unwittingly
released Elfrida there hadn't been one single minute
during which he'd been bored!

As the following day was Sunday (no special early
morning deliveries as they didn't 'do Sundays') it
meant that Roy could blissfully sleep in and, as he
and Elfrida and Granny Hatch were all rather tired,
it was a nice peaceful day which had only one rather
difficult moment in it, which was when Granny came
out early from her afternoon nap and saw Roy tip-
toeing upstairs with a very thick bacon sandwich.

'You can't *still* be hungry!' said Granny. 'You only
had your dinner an hour ago.'

'I'm always hungry,' said Roy, which was about
ninety per cent truthful.

Granny Hatch returned to her bedroom shaking her
head to herself and wondering if perhaps her grand-
son could possibly be starting to grow again.

As Mr Patrick had told them not to come to the
Library until after four o'clock on Monday afternoon
because until then he would be in charge of 'Story
Time' for younger children, Roy and Elfrida went
down to the shopping precinct with Bouncer. Granny
Hatch was both surprised and delighted when Roy
offered to take the dirty washing to the Queensam
Launderette, which had written on the window 'Come
Clean With Us'. And Mr Cliff, when asked for the
loan of Bouncer once more, said, 'Again? It's very
good of you Roy. We appreciate it, Bouncer and I.

Seemed quite a young dog last week after all that exercise. This is no place for a dog y'know. No place for older people either because nobody wants to talk to you ... no, no didn't mean that. Here's the lead. Off you go, lad.'

Elfrida was fascinated by the Precinct and, if Roy hadn't hit on the inspired idea of tying a coloured ribbon round her wrist, he would have lost track of her over and over again, as she would keep wandering off to look in all the windows. It was the grocers and the supermarkets (fortunately most of them shut as it was Monday) which she really liked and Roy had to drag the protesting Bouncer this way and that as he went chasing after Elfrida.

'Honestly,' said Roy, when they had a five minute break sitting on one of the benches in front of a small fountain, 'you're more trouble than Bouncer.'

'Is that your doggy's name then?' said the lady who was sitting on the other end of the bench as she rocked a pram backwards and forwards.

'Yes. No. That is,' said Roy.

'I wish *we* had a doggy,' said the lady, rocking harder than ever, 'but it's not easy in Queensam, because Pets Aren't Encouraged. Where we used to live in Leytonstone we had a doggy and a pussy and a budgie and a whole tank of goldfish. It's a shame really.'

'Yes,' said Roy, who wasn't at all sure what the lady meant, but who felt he ought to say something.

'In Leytonstone,' the lady went on, rocking the pram faster and faster so that it was a wonder the baby wasn't sea-sick, 'my mum and dad and all my aunties and uncles and my granny and grandfather lived ever so close by. It's not the same here is it?'

'Yes,' said Roy and then getting a very sharp dig in the ribs from Elfrida. 'That is, no.'

'That's right,' said the lady, getting to her feet. 'Well cheerio for now. I've enjoyed our chat. It's quite a while since I had a chat with anybody really. Ta-ta.'

'Ta-ta,' said Roy.

'Poor lady,' said Elfrida, 'if you've got a nice large family it must be lovely to have them in the same village with you.'

'It must *always* be all right for a Princess like you anyway,' said Roy, who felt a bit uncomfortable for some reason. 'I mean you live in a Castle with hundreds of slaves to look after you, and those great big hunting dogs for pets, and then there's the King and Queen, your father and mother, down in the Throne Room. It's O.K. for you, isn't it!'

'Oh yes, of course it is,' said Elfrida. 'It's super. Rather. Yes.' But she sounded very sad for some reason and if Roy had known exactly where her shoulders were he'd have given them an encouraging thump, only he didn't so he said the first thing which came into his head instead.

'Have a Super-Creme-Cornet, Chocolate flavour.'

It was a bad mistake for even on Mondays the Precinct was fairly full and the sight of a coloured ribbon jogging up and down within a few inches of a melting ice-cream cone, both of them about three feet off the ground, made more than one shopper stop, stare, shake their heads and then walk on trying to puzzle out what it could all be advertising.

Elfrida was unusually silent during the walk back to the Corner Stores and that gave Roy the opportunity to think over the few facts he had been able to gather about her so far. She was a Princess and she had been imprisoned in a tower of Queensam Castle, although quite *why* or by whom he hadn't yet discovered as Elfrida seemed strangely vague about these points. By some sort of luck, good or bad— he wasn't sure which yet—he had set her free and now all he had to do was to find some way of making her visible. Although how a princess, who belonged to hundreds of years ago and who wore a gold thread dress—and probably a crown—and who quite often got muddled with her words and her ideas, could possibly live in Queensam New Town without finding herself in all kinds of trouble, was just about impossible to imagine. And, what was more, she would drag him into it too and Roy went quite pale as all kinds of hideous visions flashed across his mind.

'Ooooooh, flip,' said Roy, and then he remembered Mr Hugh Patrick and that cheered him up a bit so he was able to do justice to his Granny's cheese potato pie and crunchy flan with treacle and to smuggle up rather limp portions to Elfrida.

'Great,' said Elfrida, quite obviously licking her fingers. 'Your food, though very soft and sweet, is easy to eat all right.'

'Isn't yours?' asked Roy, staring at the kitchen spoon as it wafted up and down.

'Not always,' replied Elfrida somewhat indistinctly. 'Food goes rotten so quickly and if there's no cold weather we get maggots in everything. Our sugar isn't a bit like yours and we haven't got potatoes and to keep food from going mouldy we have to use an awful lot of salt and its *so* expensive. And bear meat can be dreadfully tough.'

'*Bear* meat! There aren't any Bears here!'

'Oh yes there jolly well are. S'cuse me,' the kitchen spoon was scraped round the plate, and then apparently licked thoroughly, 'bears and wolves and foxes and boars, that's wild pigs you know, and I have heard that once upon a time there were *tigers*! But I've never quite believed *that*. What's for afters?'

Elfrida really was remarkably fast at picking up the language, but when Roy reluctantly gave her a packet of cheese and onion crisps which he'd been planning to eat in bed that evening, Elfrida almost choked over them and had to be given two mugs of water to recover because she wasn't used to so much pure salt. She was still spluttering a bit when they reported to the Library where Mr Patrick, looking paler than ever, was clearing up and pushing the chairs into tidy positions with his bony knees.

'I say, it's you, Thatch,' said Mr Patrick almost dropping his toppling pile of Beginning to Read Books. 'I really did think I'd dreamt you, you know, if that doesn't sound too rude. That is until old Wickens, sorry I mean Councillor Wickens, rang up

again to complain. You know he really doesn't like
you very much, Thatch.'

'*Hatch*, and I know he doesn't.'

'Here, what about me?' interrupted Elfrida, handing over Bouncer's lead, a proceeding which made
Mr Patrick's eyes shift from left to right and then
back again so that they looked rather like rolling
marbles behind his thick spectacles.

'Yes, can you help us, her, that is Elfrida?' asked
Roy, gently pushing Mr Patrick towards the chair
behind the desk so that the young librarian sat down
with a thud which made Bouncer look round sleepily
before once more resting his several chins on the
nice cool floor.

'Ah . . .' said Mr Patrick. 'Yes, well, that is I'm not
at all sure! '

'I've drawn you a plan,' said Elfrida. 'It's not very
good I'm afraid, but it's what Roy and me saw from
the top of your tall castle.'

'She means the Tower Block,' Roy said kindly as
Mr Patrick's marble eyes rolled faster than ever as a
somewhat creased poster—which had 'Queensam
Super-Mart Super Sale' on one side and a not very
good hand-drawn map on the other—suddenly appeared out of thin air.

'Goodness gracious me,' said Mr Patrick polishing
up his spectacles with the bottom of his sweater.
'Dear, dear, I say, well . . .'

'Does it help?' asked Elfrida, breathing so heavily
down Mr Patrick's ear that one side of his spectacles
quite misted over and had to be cleaned again. 'Oh

it's horrible being invisible all the time, please, please do something.'

'Yes, well,' said Mr Patrick pushing his fingers through his long hair so that it stood up in wavy tufts. 'I don't know that I *can* do anything really, but what you've drawn here is most interesting. It's a white magic symbol of course.'

'I wouldn't have anything to do with the *other* sort!' said Elfrida in such a shocked voice that everybody, including Bouncer, shook their heads in agreement.

'Ah yes, rather,' agreed Mr Patrick. 'Two triangles, lying across each other, that's a very old idea, older than Time itself probably, that's what brought you here er—Miss—er?'

'Elfrida. Princess actually. But that's not important now. What *does* matter is making me visible. Can you do it?'

'I? What? Who?' said Mr Patrick who was bending over the map so closely that his nose nearly touched it. 'It's not my kind of work really Lady Elfrida— what a very pretty name that is—and I haven't done much research on the subject. I mean I've not had much call for it before in the library, and anyway you know, I did think you and Thatch were all a dream, but if you *are* prepared to trust me, here goes. I say, are you?'

Roy looked at where he hoped Elfrida was sitting and apart from a faint prickling sensation in his head he really did feel both interested and excited. For after all, it would be nice to see what Elfrida looked like after having rescued her and fed her and housed her!

Bouncer opened his old eyes, yawned and then put his chins down on his paws and as for Elfrida, she was dancing from toe to toe in anticipation.

'Yes, I'll trust you,' Roy and Elfrida said together, while Bouncer snorted and snored at the same moment.

'Well I dunno,' said Mr Patrick. 'I'm sure the Council wouldn't approve of any of it, but according to this book I found in the Archives Section and this plan here and the other bits of research I've done— I say are you really *sure*?'

Everybody said they were in their separate ways and Mr Patrick who was getting less and less sure about everything every single second, got up and walked out of Queensam Library via the wide open French windows; across the rather sun-burnt grass to the edge of 'Keep Off Park' and then, as nobody else seemed to be about he skipped over the Council sign and feeling sillier by the second, he strode into the late summer mist, which was rising over the grass quite thickly by now, and he muttered the words he'd got out of the library book, while he re-crossed the lines that Roy had made on his bicycle.

And it was while Mr Patrick was re-crossing the last line of all in the soft summer haze that Roy and Elfrida and even Bouncer had a quite extraordinary feeling, as if the whole of the New Town was being pulled towards them on invisible strings and before Roy had a chance to say anything at all everything seemed to be spinning round his head and he felt rather sick and then at almost the same moment he heard a very irritable voice say,

'Well girl, don't stand there like a dolt! Perhaps you'd have the courtesy to explain who gave *you* permission to enter MY garden and furthermore, WHY are you wearing a night-dress? Well?'

It was a very bossy voice and it belonged to a very small lady with a white face and curly orange hair. She was wearing a dress with an enormous collar and a skirt so big that she was wider than she was tall, and standing in front of her was a girl of about Roy's age. She was a skinny sort of girl with a sun-burnt face and a long plait of hair and she was wearing a long greeny-grey dress with yellow embroidery which was a bit frayed round the hem and the edge of the sleeves. It looked more like a dressing-gown than a night-dress and it certainly wasn't half as smart as the pretty pink nylon housecoat that Roy's Granny had bought last Christmas at Marks and Spencer.

All this went through Roy's mind in a flash and before the girl had even answered all the cross questions, Roy realised two things. First that the girl must be Elfrida-of-the-Castle and secondly that Queensam New Town had completely vanished. Not one small corner of it remained. Instead there was a long low house with a great many windows and chimneys and with a large garden full of low, neatly cut hedges. In fact Roy was practically tripping over a hedge at this moment. To his right was an

enormous tree which was shifting and sighing in the
warm breeze, while beyond it were some grassy
mounds and the remains of a few broken down stone
walls.

It was all so interesting that Roy didn't bother to
listen to what was being said as he slowly turned on
his heel, pulling Bouncer's lead tight as he did so.
Bouncer growled at the back of his throat and the
small lady stopped waving her bony ring-covered
finger under Elfrida's nose and said sharply,

'What was that, Miss?'

'I don't know,' said Elfrida miserably. She'd had
three minutes of being told off for being in the Cross
Lady's private garden, there was no sign of Roy or
Mr Patrick or even Bouncer, she didn't know where
she was or what was happening and everything was
horrible.

'It was Bouncer, of course,' said Roy. 'Stop it, you
stupid dog!'

Elfrida and the small Cross Lady both stepped
backwards and instinctively drew closer together.

'Witchcraft!' whispered the lady. 'My enemies have
surrounded me with witchcraft, and I believed myself
safe here close to my trusty elm tree!'

'Roy,' said Elfrida, peering left and right. 'Mr
Patrick? Bouncer? Are you there?'

'Of course I'm here,' Roy began angrily, 'and
Bouncer. He's on the end ... on the end ...' Roy had
meant to say 'on the end of his lead,' but he never
finished the sentence because at that exact second
he glanced down at where he knew Bouncer was,

but there was no dog, no lead and, what was far, far worse no hand holding the lead...

Roy kicked his right foot against his left ankle and it was quite painful. Then he jumped up and down and his feet thudded against the gravel path. He could feel it happening and he could see the bits of gravel shooting off in all directions, but of his feet and indeed the rest of himself and of Bouncer and Mr Patrick there was no sign at all, and Roy shivered from the top of his head to his toes.

'Well,' said Elfrida, hitching up her skirt as she took a step forwards, 'now it's happened to *you*! Now *you* know what it's like being invisible! It's not at all nice, is it?'

'You *are* a witch, are you not?' whispered the Cross Lady. 'And you are talking to your familiars, your spirit companions. But you do not frighten ME. I shall summon my guards and have you arrested and taken away and questioned. I may even have you beheaded for treason.'

'It's not allowed by law,' said Roy. 'Not beheading, honestly it isn't. And Elfrida's too young for prison. She'd be sent to ... that is, I mean...'

'I *am* the law,' said the Cross Lady and she clapped her hands loudly, 'and I shall have all your heads, invisible or otherwise! Gentlemen, to me AT ONCE!'

There was the sound of distant voices and then running footsteps which grew closer and closer as torches flared in the falling dusk and the doors of the house were thrown open.

'Oh dear, oh dear, oh DEAR,' said Roy. 'Mr Patrick, please it's all gone wrong. There's no castle and me and Bouncer are invisible and we're all going to be in awful trouble. MR PATRICK!'

But there was no answer as the torches and the calling voices bobbed closer and closer across the formal garden to where the Cross Lady was standing with her head thrown back and her left hand pointing to Elfrida.

'On your knees, girl,' commanded the lady.

'Yes Madam,' whispered Elfrida in a trembling voice, and did as she was told.

5. *The Cross Lady*

Although being invisible is not very nice, neverthe-
less in many ways it does have its advantages as Roy
quickly discovered when he realised that he could
follow the captive Elfrida without any of the guards

being a fraction the wiser. Bouncer was something
of a problem, but as he had had rather an exhausting
day in any case, he stopped complaining after a few
seconds and allowed Roy to cradle him over one
shoulder, just giving a shiver and a snort now and
again. The only difficult moment came when Roy
passed too close to some hunting dogs which were
chained up to one side of the house and, invisible or
not, Bouncer quite obviously still had a very real
dog-smell, for the hounds began baying and throwing
themselves forwards and generally making such a fuss
that a fat man wearing a leather apron had to throw a
basinful of bones into their midst to quieten them
down.

Roy saw his chance while all this was going on and
hugging Bouncer close, he nipped round the four
gentlemen who were escorting the sniffing Elfrida and
managed to whisper in her ear.

'Oi, it's me. Don't worry, I'll get you out.'

'No you won't. They'll behead me and nobody'll
care anyway ... oh, oh, oh...' And poor Elfrida had
to hitch up the frayed sleeve of her dress to rub her
wrist across her eyes.

One of the gentlemen. who had a pleasant, sun-
burnt face and a great many wrinkles round his eyes,
said quite kindly,

'Don't fret, girl. Beheading's far better than being
burnt as a witch. It's quicker you see.'

'Ooooooh,' howled Elfrida. now having to use both
wrists. A crumpled paper tissue appeared out of the

dusk and she seized hold of it and blew her nose noisily.

'That was a good trick,' the gentleman said admiringly. 'Are you really a witch then, girl? It's a pity you've got across HER because SHE's not above enjoying an evening's entertainment of magic tricks. Perhaps I'll be able to talk her round. Do you do any other acts? Sawing the lady in half perhaps—oh sorry. Very tactless.'

'Tell him you can do a vanishing act,' muttered Roy out of the corner of his mouth as he retreated backwards into the house ahead of Elfrida. She repeated his words between sniffs and the gentleman laughed loudly and then put his arm round Elfrida's cold shoulders and said to his companions,

'All right gentlemen, I'll see this little lady to her quarters. She won't vanish with me about, I can assure you.'

'All right m'lord,' one of the men said reluctantly. 'But if anything should go wrong on your head be it.'

'I've felt the shadow of the axe a few times in my life. Once more won't hurt. Come along girl.'

Roy had been very much afraid that Elfrida was going to be locked away in a deep, dark dungeon, but instead of taking her downstairs the gentleman, after chewing heavily at his lower lip and fingering his square cut beard said suddenly,

'Come on, it's worth a try. SHE's not so bad really, just rather touchy and if you can do that trick with the handkerchief again SHE might just find it in her heart to forgive and forget. Now stop sniffing, child, and put out your tongue.'

And the gentleman produced a slightly grey, but very beautifully embroidered handkerchief from his padded doublet and held it out to Elfrida who did as she was told. And when the gentleman had got a corner of the handkerchief damp enough he cleaned the tear stains off Elfrida's freckled face. Then he combed her hair neatly away from her forehead, turned back her sleeves so that the shabby cuffs didn't show so much and finally he put one finger under her chin and tilted it up as he said,

'Come now, child, smile. The world's a sad old place right enough, but not at your age, eh?'

'It—it can be,' said Elfrida and gave a kind of snort and then, to Roy's astonishment, Elfrida-of-the-Castle seized hold of the red-faced gentleman's hand and shook it hard as she said in a muffled sort of way, 'I wish you had been my Dad.'

'Yes, it wouldn't have been a bad arrangement ... now then, no more tears. SHE hates people crying and who can blame her? There's been enough crying in HER life, what with one thing and another. Now you're looking very fine and you're a pretty enough child so forget about being a witch and all that nonsense and go and do a few of your conjuring tricks, and if you make HER laugh there'll be no more talk of beheadings, you'll see!'

'Yes—well—Roy?' said Elfrida turning on her heel.

Roy, who had been watching and listening and

desperately trying to understand what was happening while at the same time stroking Bouncer to stop him snoring, shuffled forward and whispered.

'I'm here. I've only got one more tissue though, apart from...' and Roy hunted desperately through the pockets of his invisible jeans realising as he did so just how difficult life must have been for Elfrida when *she* was invisible in the middle of Queensam New Town. By touch he discovered several pieces of string, some elastic bands, two old biros, his library card, half a packet of chewing gum, a very small piece of rubber, a football lace, three cards out of a breakfast cereal and half a sparkler which must have been nestling at the very bottom of this particular pocket for nearly ten months.

'Flip,' said Roy. 'Apart from, hang on ... I say, Elfrida, I don't know if it'll help, but if there's any kind of fire going you start talking about it and I'll chuck in this firework and perhaps they'll stop looking at you for a few seconds and we'll get away. O.K.?'

'O.K.,' whispered Elfrida, adding, 'I don't like it. I don't like any of it and where's Sir Patrick gone?'

'Vanished for ever, I suppose. Good luck, and I'm sorry, I didn't understand before about how difficult it was being invisible. Shake on it?'

'That's all right,' said Elfrida in a brave voice, but her hand was as cold as a packet of frozen chips straight out of the Corner Store's deep freeze, and her teeth were chattering so much that she almost bit her tongue.

'That's enough of that,' said the stout gentleman who had been combing his hair and beard with the aid of a polished silver hand mirror. He flicked up the frills of his beautiful starched ruff, pulled down his doublet and then crooked his finger at Elfrida to come and join him. 'Well, girl, and what tricks shall I announce first eh?'

'Silver stars,' whispered Roy.

'S-s-silver stars,' repeated Elfrida.

'What a very odd sounding trick that is. Well, well let us hope that it will amuse HER. Wait a moment child, while I look through a crack in the door. Yes, yes, SHE has changed her sleeves and ruff and she looks altogether much happier than she was. Hold on while I go and have a word with the musicians.'

The stout gentleman eased his way into what appeared to be a much larger room for a great hum of voices and some rather discordant music could be heard. There was also a strong smell of food which made Elfrida breathe deeply and quite forget for a few seconds that she was in very great danger and which also, rather unfortunately, roused Bouncer from his nap. The voice of the stout gentleman was just saying,

'... now then, now then, My Pretty, you can remember what it's like to be an orphan child can't you? It wasn't so long ago after all...'

'Oh Robin, Robin,' said the Cross Lady, only now she was smiling so she sounded quite different, 'what tales are you about to spin me?'

'No tale, My Pretty, I only wish to present to you some small entertainment which will keep you amused. That orphan child was no witch, merely a child trying to learn her trade as a conjuror—a trade which I very much fear she has only just begun to practise. Her performance will probably be dreadfully bad, but please, My Pretty, do not hiss and boo too loudly. Promise?'

'Robin, Robin,' the lady began shaking her head and smiling more than ever, 'very well, bring on this orphan child and...'

Everything now appeared to be going so well that Roy quite forgot to be careful, with the result that Bouncer had no trouble at all in suddenly heaving himself out of Roy's arms, scrambling heavily to the ground and then lurching through the half open door and into the big room in search of that delicious smelling food.

'Bouncer, to heel,' shouted Roy running after him. Elfrida, although she had more than enough to worry about, realised at once what was happening, which was more than anybody else did, of course. All the splendidly dressed people who were sitting round a table which was shaped like three sides of a square, saw was a scared freckle-faced girl standing in the doorway, twisting a fold of her shabby dress between her fingers. *That* wasn't interesting enough to make them stop talking for a second, but when a serving man who was about to put down a plate with a sizzling joint of meat on it, suddenly lost his balance for no reason at all so that the joint shot into the air,

and then that very same joint began to race round
the room a few inches from the ground, it was a very
different matter. The voices all stopped at once,
some of the gentlemen scrambled to their feet and
leant forward on the table so that they could follow
the progress of the joint as it careered round and
round, and several of the ladies put their hands over
their eyes and tried to pretend that nothing unusual
was going on.

The kind-gentleman-called-Robin staggered back
with his hands behind him as the joint raced past
his knees, and the Cross Lady leant across the table
and whacked his knuckles with the first thing which
came to hand which happened to be an enormous
serving spoon.

'Witchcraft!' she said furiously. '*Just* as I suspected
all along. Well, I won't stand for it, do you hear!
Bring that loin of beef to me IMMEDIATELY.'

And down came the serving spoon again, a split
second after Robin managed to get his fingers out
of the way. His face had gone quite pale under his
tan and Elfrida suddenly forgot to be scared out of
her wits as she remembered how kind he had been to
her. She marched across the room as the meat came
round on its third circuit and said very loudly,
'Bouncer! To heel. Drop it!'

The invisible Bouncer skidded to a halt and actually did as he was told, so that Roy, who was about
three strides behind him, tripped and landed with
a painful 'Ouch' on his hands and knees and with a
crash that seemed to make the teeth rattle in his

head. It also dislodged his plastic library card from the pocket of his jeans so that it shot across the polished floor and vanished from sight.

'You're a naughty, naughty dog,' said Elfrida and she picked up the slightly chewed joint of meat and hurried across to the serving man who all this time had been sitting on the polished floor with both his eyes and his mouth as round as buttons, and with a muttered 'excuse me, please', she borrowed the cloth he was still feebly holding in one hand and, wrapping it smartly round the chewed bit, she slid the meat back on to its plate and presented it to the kind gentleman in such a professional way that he accepted it without thinking.

'THERE,' said Elfrida, 'most of it's still perfectly all right to eat you know. But I don't suppose it's very hot now so you'd better carve as quickly as you can. It'd be a shame to waste such a lovely joint, wouldn't it?'

As Elfrida finished speaking she realised that everyone, even the invisible Roy and Bouncer, were apparently holding their respective breaths while all of them stared at her. It was a most embarrassing experience and Elfrida's pale face slowly began to grow pinker and pinker so that her freckles disappeared entirely.

'Are you or are you not a witch?' asked the Cross Lady, leaning so far forward on the table and speaking with such a hissing sort of voice that Elfrida took half a step backwards.

'Course I'm not,' Elfrida replied. 'I'm just looking

for my own castle so that I can go home again and be safe.'

'Treason! I thought so! I suspected it all the time! An orphan girl indeed! You and your soft tongue, Robin, it'll be the death of you yet! Guards, guards, clap the girl in irons and be quick about it! There's no castle hereabouts that belongs to anyone but ME. Why, all of this part of the country is MINE and always has been, guarded over by MY elm tree...'

'Steady on, Bess,' said Robin regaining both his tongue and his balance.

'Don't you "Bess" me,' snapped the lady, 'or I'll have you put in the Tower for disrespect, d'you hear!' And down came the spoon again with such a thud that it got a nasty dent.

Roy, who was just about getting his breath back from his fall, was at his wit's end as to what to do next, for the whole situation was now taking on nightmarish proportions with the all too visible Elfrida in even worse trouble than she had been twenty minutes ago. Roy decided that the only course left to him was to abandon all hope of finding Mr Patrick and to leave him to his fate. Elfrida, now having a head which was quite obviously attached to a neck (which was of course attached to her shoulders), might very well be in danger of the axe doing a great deal of *de*-taching, as the Cross Lady was now looking extremely determined while the kind gentleman's complexion resembled a bottle of milk. Elfrida, therefore, had to be rescued from the slowly approaching pike-staffs of the guards who luckily appeared to be rather reluctant to get too close to her.

'Oh flip, here goes,' muttered Roy, and he made a grab for the growling Bouncer with one hand and with the other he pulled the dusty sparkler out of his pocket and thrust it into the nearest candle flame. It was rather an old firework and the inside of Roy's pocket must have been a bit damp for nothing happened at all. Roy's right hand began to shake with agitation and his left arm started to ache with the strain of holding on to Bouncer, who was a large, heavy dog and was once again straining to get at that delicious food.

'Help me, help me, oh please, please help me,' whispered Elfrida, her freckles looking like brown dots on her white face.

'I'm doing my best,' muttered Roy. 'When this firework catches light I'll hand it to you, and you wave it round and round and make some sort of loud noise and with any luck they'll be so scared for a sec or two that you'll be able to make a dash for it . . . O.K.?'

'Yes, no, oh dear, oh dear.'

'Come ON. Catch fire DO. Bouncer stop wriggling. OH!'

Roy was not the only person to say 'OH' for while the sparkler was still sulkily doing nothing, the candle flame flickered sideways until it was parallel with the top of the table, and so did all the other candles, for a sudden chill wind had sprung up as the door was thrown open with a crash and a figure appeared. A man was standing in the doorway with his arms folded across his chest and a most disagreeable expression on his round, red face. He was wearing what looked to Roy like a long dark dressing-gown with a hood attached and leathery flip-flop slippers. He was also faintly familiar and then Roy realised that this was the man who had thrown the bones to the growling dogs earlier.

'Now WHAT?' demanded the Cross Lady, raising the dented serving spoon slightly.

'Madam, it is ME,' said the fat gentleman.

'You fool, you idiot, you dolt, I can see that it's you! I've got eyes in my head—front and back—now shut that door for goodness sake. This hall is full of draughts enough as it is!'

'Madam, I obey your command. BUT first let me get rid of that young sorceress, that young witch who wishes YOU Madam, so much evil!'

'I don't,' Elfrida began indignantly. 'I never saw this lady before in my life and ... oh...' And Elfrida went even more white and stepped back right on Roy's toe, which, invisible or not, still hurt.

'Exactly, precisely, now we're getting down to it,' said the fat man rubbing his podgy hands together. 'You recognise me all right, don't you miss? Oh no! Don't think you'll get away from me so easily as all that! Let me tell you miss, that I don't start training young...'

Everybody's heads were now turning from left to right and back again from the chalk-faced Elfrida, who looked as though she was about to burst into tears at any minute, to the podgy man as they talked backwards and forwards. Even the Cross Lady and Roy, let alone the guards, were so intrigued, that it came as a great surprise when the sparkler at long last burst into life and went off with a most satisfying fizz and a great burst of blue-white stars. Roy very nearly dropped it and then somehow managed to thrust it into Elfrida's cold and shaking hand and grasping her firmly by the wrist he shouted at the top of his voice.

'ONE, TWO, THREE!
THE FOOTBALL TEAM FOR ME...
QUEENS*AM—UNITED*!'

And somehow he managed to push her ahead of him still shouting and the circle of guards with their lowered pikestaffs shifted and moved and then broke, leaving a small gap.

'Guards, guards,' shouted the shrill voice of the small Cross Lady.

'Don't let her go...' roared the podgy man.

'Get on, get on,' implored Roy, pushing and shoving with all his might.

'Woof, woof, woof,' yelped Bouncer struggling and wriggling as hard as he could.

'Oh, oh, oh, help,' shrieked Elfrida, holding the spluttering sparkler at arm's length with her eyes half shut.

'What a wonderful performance,' said the kind gentleman, whose face had become quite pink again. 'You must admit, lovey, that it's the best conjuring trick YOU'VE ever seen!'

'*I* admit nothing,' said the Cross Lady. 'I never

have and I never shall. But what was Old Wick...'

And then her voice was cut off as the big door slammed shut behind Roy, Elfrida and the wriggling Bouncer, and for a moment there was nothing to be seen but the faint fizzing stars of the sparkler which were growing paler every second.

'Now what happens?' asked Elfrida.

And out of the darkness a voice said,

'Oh, hallo, is that you? I say, what a quite extraordinary...'

'Mr Patrick.'

'Sir Patrick,' shouted Roy and Elfrida together and even Bouncer managed a deep bark. And somehow in a muddled kind of way, all three of them managed to get across the idea that it was more than time that they all of them got out of their present predicament.

'Oh,' said the voice of the invisible Mr Patrick, 'is it? should we? But, *why*? It's very interesting, you know. I've been studying the origin of the Queen's Elm, its that big tree over there.'

'If you don't get us away ever so quickly,' panted Roy, 'we'll all be swinging from its branches, if we're invisible or not. *You* got us here, now get us OUT!'

Mr Patrick seemed to hesitate for a second or two and then the door of the big house swung open, letting out a stream of light and the sound of a great many agitated voices plus the baying of a pack of hounds.

'Get on QUICK,' shouted Roy.

Mr Patrick appeared to grab the now dying sparkler

from Elfrida and to wave some kind of pattern in
the dark starlight air, gabbling as he did so. Elfrida
was inside the sparkling pattern of light and so was
Roy, but Bouncer chose to take this last chance to try
and wriggle free and then Roy tightened his grip and
everything seemed to slip sideways and to whirl
round and round and when he managed to open
his eyes again he found that he was sitting on a green
mound with a very pasty-faced Mr Patrick beside him
and a struggling Bouncer in his arms.

Several large cars and two minibuses squealed
round the green mound and Roy took several deep
breaths and looked up and around and saw that
he was surrounded by the towers of Queensam New
Town. After what he had been through they seemed
quite reassuringly solid.

'Oh glory,' said Roy, 'that was close, eh? Elfrida,
where are you?'

'Here,' said the shaking voice of Elfrida, 'I'm *here*,
Roy. And thank you ever so much for rescuing me.
Am I invisible again?'

Roy looked left and right and then nodded sadly,
for there was nothing to be seen but the last of the
clover and the yellowy-green of the grass.

'Ahhhhh, ooooh,' said Elfrida. 'I see. It was ... he
was ... she was... Never mind. It's ever so nice to be
back, really. But there is *one* small thing. Have you
looked at Bouncer properly?'

Roy and Mr Patrick pulled themselves together
and tried very hard to concentrate. There was the
grass and the traffic and Roy and Bouncer, but...

'Oh *dear*!' said Mr Patrick, 'I don't understand any of it and I don't know what's happened or how we've got back or even where we've *been*, come to that, but that dog only has two and a half legs . . .'

'Woof, woof, woof,' agreed Bouncer, 'woof.'

6. The Disappearing Dog

Escaping from the sixteenth century with all its guards and its constant threats of either being imprisoned or beheaded was really quite simple in a way when compared to getting one boy, one white-faced Junior

Librarian, one mongrel dog with one and a half invisible legs and a totally invisible princess off a traffic island roundabout in a New Town. It didn't help that the rush hour had started so that cars, vans, lorries and buses were nose to tail as everybody made for the Motorway. Elfrida, who had never before been so close to so much noise and speed, sank back against Mr Patrick's shoulder and heaved an enormous sigh which was part relief and part tiredness and part fear at yet another new enemy to vanquish.

'Chuck up, chicken,' said Mr Patrick who, as he was now convinced that he had gone quite mad, had decided to enjoy whatever happened next, because it was all far more exciting and interesting than anything that had ever happened to him before in his not very long life.

'What does that mean?' asked Elfrida.

'It means cheer up and stop worrying so much. The Matron at the Home used to say it to me.'

'Was she your mother?'

'No, no. I was what we call an orphan. When I was a very small baby I was left in a shopping bag, from Marks and Spencer I believe it was, on a railway station on St Patrick's Day which is how I got my name.'

'If you don't mind,' interrupted Roy, 'I think it's about time we got off here and back home, otherwise Granny'll start creating. Worrying,' he added hastily as he heard Elfrida draw in her breath to ask a question. But in fact what she was doing was giving a most tremendous yawn which, although invisible, infected everybody else including Bouncer who yawned wider and more loudly than anybody, after which he scratched himself vigorously with one of his invisible legs.

'It was all my fault,' said Mr Patrick, watching this very odd looking behaviour. 'I suppose he was just that little bit outside the signs I was drawing, just as you and I were, Roy, at the start of the spell ... I can only say that all this magic stuff is new to me, which is why I'm not very good at it.'

'Never mind,' said Elfrida kindly. 'I always got bored in magic classes. I wish I *had* listened more carefully though, because learning things does seem to come in useful after all.'

'HOW ARE WE GOING TO GET OFF THIS ROUNDABOUT?' asked Roy, who was learning very fast indeed that the only way to get Elfrida and Mr Patrick to do anything was to shout.

The following half-an-hour was so nightmarish and noisy with drivers swerving and shouting and shaking their fists and sounding their horns every time when either Roy or Mr Patrick so much as put one foot off the grass and on to the road, that it looked as if they might be stuck on their island all night. However, luckily for them a policeman came swooping round on his motor-cycle and, after one glance at the tired, white-faced man and boy, he stopped his engine, held up the traffic, gave Mr Patrick a short, sharp lecture on pedestrian behaviour and waved them on their way.

It wasn't until some time later that the same police-man, who felt that something had been puzzling away at the back of his mind, stopped his cycle again, turned down his radio and muttered to himself.

'Did I dream it—or did that dog only have two and a half legs? No...! All the same there *was* something very odd about those people. I think I'll just go back and take another look...'

He was young and he was anxious to make a success of his job, and so he took the trouble to make a proper search of the area round the roundabout, and as it was dark by now his torch, when flashed over a barrier which was set well back from the road and which had a large notice on it saying COUNCIL PROPERTY KEEP OFF, just happened to show up something small and white. It was Roy's library ticket, the self-same ticket which had slipped out of Roy's pocket in the Manor House dining-room.

'Well, well, well, *tres*passers. I thought as much,' said the young policeman (quite untruthfully) and he slid the library card into his pocket and kicked his bike into action and went zooming off into the dark warm night.

Meanwhile Roy, who was so tired he could hardly stand upright, was trying to explain to a somewhat puzzled Mr Cliff that Bouncer was perfectly all right, but because they'd been for such a long walk (quite true) he was now exhausted and had gone fast asleep (partly true) so please could he, Bouncer, stay the night at the Corner Stores?

'I suppose so,' said Mr Cliff. 'He *is* rather old, in

fact he's *very* old. Between you and me, Roy, I don't know what we'll do when Bouncer dies.... We're very fond of him, you know. He's really all we've got left in the world since our niece went away, what would it be? Ten—no nearer twelve years ago now. She was a sweet girl, Annie was, more like a daughter than a niece, but she didn't take to Queensam, said it was too dull for her. And now Annie's been dead this long time and there's me and Mrs Cliff with just Bouncer to worry about...'

'If—if anything ever happened to Bouncer,' said Roy, who in spite of being stiff all over from tiredness now felt worse than ever about those one-and-a-half invisible legs after hearing Mr Cliff's sad story, 'couldn't you, couldn't you get another dog? A whole dog—I mean,' he added hastily, 'a young dog. A puppy!'

'We could, but I don't suppose we *would*. Dogs aren't welcome here as I've said many a time. It's "keep off the grass" and "no dogs allowed" and all the rest of it, and if you use your eyes, young Roy, you'll see as how they're precious few dogs around the place these days. Well, well off you go now, you looks as if you're asleep on your feet. Give my regards to your grandmother and I'll expect Bouncer back when I see him. Let him sleep poor old chap and see that he has a bowl of water...'

The problems now facing Roy were so enormous that he decided that the only thing he could do was to forget all about them until tomorrow. Elfrida was still completely invisible, Bouncer was invisible

in parts, Mr Patrick—although a grown-up—seemed
to be getting very dreamy and funny in the head
judging by the way he had wandered off muttering
and whispering to himself and doing a kind of skipping dance into the darkness; and, apart from all that,
it hadn't been very nice being transported backwards
in time to a place where being beheaded or threatened or even just imprisoned seemed to be quite the
usual run of things. Added to which, thought Roy,
thumping away at his pillow, he was starting to be
pretty suspicious about Elfrida herself. He had a
sneaking feeling that she hadn't been telling him the
real truth. There were clues everywhere, but at this
particular moment he couldn't be bothered to work
them out properly . . .

Roy was still feeling rather muddled in the head
when he set off on his early morning paper round.
Once again it was fairly misty and Roy zigzagged
backwards and forwards with Bouncer bouncing
and barking behind the bike and really behaving a
great deal younger than his age. Bouncer hadn't
felt so fit for a long while and as he hadn't noticed
that part of himself was invisible he hadn't a worry
in the world.

'How,' said Roy, delivering the *Daily Telegraph*
and *The Sun* to No. 12 Acorn Street, 'how can you
possibly make invisible people visible again? When
we went back to wherever it was *I* wasn't there
but Elfrida *was*. How do you get things to work
out right at the same time?'

'Woof, woof, woof,' barked Bouncer happily

dodging in and out of the mist.

'And how am I going to explain YOU?' asked Roy, sliding the *Daily Express*, *The Times* and a magazine through the next letter-box.

'Woof,' agreed Bouncer.

'Oh shut UP.'

'You're looking very pale, dear,' said Granny Hatch at breakfast time, 'I've always thought that we'd taken on too many morning papers. I hope you're not overdoing it. And what's more ...'

And Granny Hatch pushed back her chair and trotted round the kitchen table and prodded Roy in the ribs while she looked him up and down, over and under her spectacles.

'What is it?' asked Roy uneasily.

'You look—you look—um—I dunno,' muttered his Granny, 'different, that's all. Oh botheration there goes the shop bell. I'm coming, I'm coming. Roy, get on with the washing up, dear. Oh, good morning Mrs Swift, and how's the world treating you today?'

Roy took the chance to pile three slices of toast, a large dollop of Marmite and an apple on to a plate and then he hurried up the stairs to where Elfrida, with Bouncer now lolling beside her, was still fast asleep. He was in such a hurry that he hit the top of his head on a low beam and for a moment he quite literally saw stars.

'Morning,' said the voice of Elfrida as the sleeping bag stirred, 'Oh *food*! Goody.'

Breakfast vanished in a matter of a very few

minutes and then the sleeping bag flattened out and the attic window misted over as Elfrida looked out across Queensam.

'What happens next?' asked Elfrida, drawing patterns on the misty glass.

'I think,' said Roy, folding his arms and sitting down with his back to the door, 'I think you'd better tell me all the truth.'

'Yes, well,' Elfrida's invisible finger-nail scrabbled against the glass in a way which made Bouncer suddenly wake up with his ears back. 'Well, you see I was, I mean I am Elfrida-of-the-Castle...'

'*Why* were your made invisible?'

'I didn't do my lessons properly, and I ate rather a lot.'

'What lessons?'

'Lessons in magic. They were ever so dull, you know.'

'WHO made you become invisible and WHY?'

'It was old Wickery,' said Elfrida in a sulky voice, 'he's the one that's supposed to teach all the—that is everybody in Form One, magic, and he was always ever so cross and boring and dull. *I* wanted to learn cooking and herb planting and cleaning and laundry work, all the *interesting* things, but old Wickery, *he* wouldn't let me. So he got crosser and crosser and in the end, when I hadn't done my homework on some stupid old spell or other, he just got ever so angry and I got invisible. All right?'

'No, not really,' said Roy, thinking this over, 'because what about your parents? The King and

Queen, your father and mother. They must've been jolly angry about your vanishing.'

'Ah,' said Elfrida, the window misting up more than ever, 'them! Yes! Well! They *were* dreadfully angry, but there wasn't much they could do about it as Old Wickery was so powerful. I mean a court magician *is* tremendously important.'

'But,' said Roy, wrinkling up his forehead, 'you told that fat, jolly man we met yesterday, that you'd have liked *him* to be your father so...'

'Oh shut up,' said Elfrida furiously and the copy of *Queensam! What's On!* suddenly travelled across the attic and hit Roy quite hard on the head.

'Oi, watch it.'

'Sorry. I know you rescued me all over again yesterday and I *am* ever so grateful, really, but please don't keep *on* asking questions.'

'All right, all right, calm down,' said Roy hastily as Elfrida sniffed violently. 'But what happens next about Bouncer? I *can't* take him back to Mr Cliff with half his legs missing. I suppose it'll mean having to get Mr Patrick to do his magic again and hoping for the best, but he doesn't seem very good at it. Can't *you* remember any of the magic that you were taught at school?'

'Only bits and pieces like taking small spells off people and listening to things which are a long way-away. I was ever so glad that I'd learnt *that* bit because it was awfully dull being stuck inside the invisible castle. Nobody ever came near to me and I'd've got dreadfully lonely if I hadn't listened in to people walking past the edge of the Park sometimes.'

'Well, that's no help,' said Roy gloomily.

'I did get to Upper Two in flying,' suggested Elfrida, 'but you need a broomstick for that really. There was one girl in our class who could fly dreadfully well. She said that she was going to give up cooking and laundry and become a proper Witchwise-woman, but it takes years and years to get your "W" Levels and anyway some people have to start work quite young.'

'What sort of work?' asked Roy. 'I'm going to take some "O" Levels, but I can do a paper round and deliveries in my time off and in the holidays. Is it different for you?'

'Sort of,' said Elfrida, making a noise as if she was rubbing her feet together. 'Roy, there's something I'd like to tell you about.'

And then Granny Hatch called up the stairs to say that the milkman was coming and would Roy get an extra silver-top, please, as they seemed to be getting through a lot more milk recently.

Roy went charging down with Bouncer treading on his heels just as Mr Wickens's milk float drew up with a quiet hiss and Mr Wickens in his striped apron climbed down from the driving seat, his mouth as usual turned down like a shovel as he glowered at Roy.

'I say, Mr Wickens,' said Roy.

'I want a word with you, and it's *Councillor*

Wickens, I'll have you remember. What have you got to say about this, eh?'

And Mr Wickens produced Roy's library card and flourished it under Roy's surprised nose.

'It's my ...'

'I know what it is! But it's where it was found that's interesting. You were trespassing again, weren't you? Oh no, don't bother to deny it. This library card of yours was brought to me last night by the Police.'

'Where—where was it found?'

'Oh ho! As though you didn't know! Discovered down by the workings for the new Council buildings it was. You must have sneaked under the barrier as bold as brass. What were you after? What were you up to? WHAT WERE YOU DOING?'

Roy's brain completely refused to think. All he had was a confused memory that something had slipped out of his pocket during the scene when he had been trying to rescue Elfrida from the Cross Lady's guards.

'Oh—you mean I dropped it in the banqueting hall place!' exclaimed Roy, 'where all the ladies and gentlemen were going to have their dinners. It was ...'

'Cheek!' roared Mr Wickens, going so red in the face, he resembled an over-ripe tomato. 'I'll have no more of your impudence, do you hear! I'll ...'

And then Mr Wickens caught sight of Bouncer who was coming up the road on his two and a half legs and Mr Wickens went from red to purple to pale grey, just like a traffic light does (only with different colours), and he stepped backwards with his arms outspread, very much as the nice gentleman had done, and Elfrida, who had chosen to step behind him at that particular second, got her foot trodden on extremely heavily.

'Don't, OUCH. GET OFF!' shouted Elfrida.

If Mr Wickens hadn't always been so unpleasant, not just to Roy, but also to every other young person in Queensam and quite a lot of the old ones as well, Roy might have felt sorry for him now. But then he remembered how Mr Wickens was always bullying somebody or getting another Keep Off or Keep Out notice put up so he didn't say anything at all. The ticket slid out of Mr Wickens's fingers and then got very dirty tyre marks on it as Mr Wickens drove his float over it and went off down the road and round the corner without so much as a backward glance.

'Bother,' said Roy, picking up the ticket and wiping it on his sleeve, 'I forgot to ask him for the extra pint of silver top. Instead of everything getting better it's getting worse and worse. There's you being all invisible and Bouncer being a bit invisible and me being told off for trespassing and Granny short of milk.'

'Never mind,' said Elfrida, who now Roy was in a bad mood was in a good one herself, 'we'll go and see Sir Patrick, HE'LL sort it all out. Just get some money from your Gran and we'll do the shopping after we've been to the library. O.K.?'

But even Elfrida's high spirits fell slightly when a strange young lady at the library said irritably,

'Mr Patrick isn't in today. It's all most inconvenient, as it was supposed to be my day off. Why one should allow oneself to be called in to do relief work at a second's notice I really don't know. Frankly I think it's too bad.'

She went on like this for some time as she went 'thump thump thump' with a rubber stamp on a great pile of library books.

'I'm sorry,' said Roy when at last the young lady ran out of words and all the books had been stamped, 'I mean, I'm sorry to ask, but I would like to see Sir, that is, Mr Patrick if possible. On business.'

'He resides,' said the young lady, sweeping another great pile of books towards her and resetting her rubber stamp, 'he resides at No. 2 Acorn Lane, but if he's too ill to come in to work—and I was *promised* today off—then I doubt very much if he'll be well enough to see any visitors. HM!'

'See,' whispered Elfrida, once they were well clear of the library, 'everybody in your Time is always angry or upset about something.'

'They weren't very happy in your Time!'

'But it *wasn't* My Time. It was the Wrong Time. And anyway the Nice Gentleman was very nice indeed. Is this Acorn Lane? It doesn't look much like a lane to me.'

She was quite right for it was a long, narrow, straight road with rows and rows of low rise flats, all of them exactly the same, on either side.

Nobody answered the ring on the bell at Number Two for a long time and then there were shuffling footsteps and the pale face of Mr Patrick appeared.

When he saw who was standing outside he became paler than ever and tried to shut the door again, but Roy had already got his foot in the way and so the two of them struggled for a moment and then Mr Patrick flapped a hand and said feebly,

'Go away, go away, go away ... it was all very well catching a glimpse of the past, but enough is enough.'

'You were as happy as anything last evening,' said Elfrida, adding her weight to Roy's so that the door opened slowly as Mr Patrick fell back. 'You were skipping and dancing and singing...'

'*Then* it was like a wonderful dream,' said Mr Patrick, sitting down on the bottom stair as Roy and Elfrida entered the small hall. '*There* I was in the Queensam of Good Queen Bess, Elizabeth the First, you understand.'

'Was that the Cross Lady?' asked Roy with interest. 'Glory, I never realised that. She wasn't wearing a crown and she was ever so small. Much smaller than me. Gosh!'

'Was she Queen of all the Kingdoms?' asked Elfrida who, of course, had never heard of this important lady before.

'Oh yes—well some of them,' agreed Mr Patrick. 'To be quite honest my history is a little bit misty in parts. But she was a most remarkable Queen, there's no doubt about that. Added to which I actually climbed the Great Elm which gives this town its name. Queens Elm has, you see, been shortened into Queensam over the years.'

'So that's what you were doing! Climbing trees while we—well Elfrida—almost got beheaded! You were having a nice time and we were having a nasty one!' said Roy furiously.

'It's a nasty one now for me,' said Mr Patrick, starting to hump himself backwards up the stairs, 'because when it was all a wonderful dream I enjoyed it. But then I woke up this morning and there were scratches on my hands that I'd got from climbing up the tree. I suddenly realised that everything that had happened REALLY HAD HAPPENED and I was sick. Just like that.'

'I'm sorry about that,' said Roy, wondering as he did so how many more times he was going to use those very words when really he had done nothing to make him apologise to anyone. 'But the trouble is you didn't do the spell right or something and now Bouncer's got one and a half legs missing. Please, and it really is awfully important because Bouncer's just got to go back to Mr Cliff by about dinner-time, please will you get the other one and a half legs back?'

Mr Patrick looked at Roy and then at Bouncer who was now dozing flat on his stomach in the small hall. Mr Patrick pushed his fingers through his hair, put his hands over his face, drew in a deep, deep breath and then while everyone else held theirs he said in a whisper. 'Oh dear, oh dear, oh dear ... OH DEAR. Yes, I suppose I *must*! Come on then, let's go into the other room where I've got that book with the spells in it. Though where or how I'm going to find a spell that will make one and half legs of a dog visible, I don't know.'

'Woof,' said Bouncer and scrambling up on his two and a half legs, he led the way.

7. *The Second Spell*

Whether it was because Mr Patrick wasn't feeling at all well or whether it was because, as he had said over and over again that he just wasn't very good at magic, what now happened in the lounge at No. 2

Acorn Lane was really most unfortunate.

'I don't like it,' said Mr Patrick, looking out of the side of his eyes at Bouncer who was sniffing round the three piece suite in a suspicious manner. 'I really don't think I can.'

'You MUST,' said Roy, who was starting to learn very fast that it was no good giving in to people all the time just because they happened to be bigger than you. If you were sure that what you were doing was the right thing then you had to hang on to that and put your foot down about it.

'O.K., very well,' said Mr Patrick with a deep sigh. He ran his fingers across the strings of a guitar which was leaning up against the wall of the neat little room, and then hastily stilled the rather pleasant sound he had produced.

'I say,' said Elfrida, her voice full of admiration, 'can you play the lute properly?'

'It's a guitar actually, well that's a sort of lute, I suppose. Yes I can. I took a postal course, but my landlady doesn't like me playing even softly. She says it disturbs the neighbours...'

'Think of Bouncer!' said Roy so sternly that both Mr Patrick and Bouncer himself came to attention and then Mr Patrick flipped through his library books on magic, groaned under his breath, muttered something about, 'Salt, I suppose would be the best thing,' and went blundering off to return a moment later with a packet which had 'Supers' Best Table Salt' written on the side.

'I can't think what my landlady will say,' muttered

Mr Patrick. 'Or the Borough Librarian come to that! He never did like me much ... oh well, oh dear, come on then.'

'Not back to the Cross Lady please,' said the voice of Elfrida, 'because I don't want to go to prison, or be beheaded or anything, O.K.?'

'All right,' agreed Mr Patrick, skimming through the pages of the library book, with a packet of salt tucked under his arm. 'Of course the obvious thing to do is get you back to your Right Time, Elfrida. We fell a bit short on the last occasion. I suppose you don't know what your date is? I mean where you belong in History?'

There was a short silence.

'Go ON,' said Roy, who was far more worried about Bouncer at this particular moment than he was about Elfrida.

'I *did* go on, I shook my head, didn't I?' Elfrida snapped back. And then added, 'Oh flip, of course, you can't see me do it can you? No, I don't know my Right Date. Old Wickery never taught us things like that. I think he didn't taught us because he didn't know himself, but I do know this, we were all told that the Good King, The Great-General-From-the-West was coming to take care of us.'

'But your father is the King,' said Roy, becoming interested in spite of his other problems.

'Yes, well, but only a *little* sort of king you see,' said Elfrida, obviously bouncing up and down on the sofa as the springs began to make a twanging noise.

'What Good King can she mean?' asked Roy.

'Wenceslas?' said Mr Patrick, starting to chuckle and beginning to look better altogether. 'Honestly, Roy, it's no good asking me! We'll have to try pot luck, I suppose. Say, about five hundred years before Queen Elizabeth the First? That'd take us back to William the Conqueror and although I've never heard him called the Good King exactly, at *least* there were castles in those days and the girls wore the kind of dress that Elfrida does. I suppose it's worth a try and as long as Bouncer stays inside the circle— hang on to his collar will you—I suppose with a lot of luck we might get all of her and the rest of him back again . . .'

'O.K.,' said Roy. 'Bouncer, here boy! And please don't anybody go off and climb trees or get taken prisoner or anything. We'll all stick closely together, right?'

'Right,' said Mr Patrick and Elfrida together and even Bouncer managed a kind of yawning growl and Mr Patrick started to draw a pattern with the cooking salt on the carpet and everything was going very well when there was a sudden pitter-patter of footsteps up the front path and the sound of a key in the front door.

'Oh goodness, it's my landlady,' said Mr Patrick, stopping in his tracks.

'Are you there?' called a voice, and Bouncer recognising that voice, gave a bound forwards with his tail wagging in greeting, Roy made a grab for Bouncer's long white fur and just managed to get hold of it, but Bouncer had already managed to jog Mr Patrick's elbow and a great cloud of salt rose up in the air and as the smiling if rather puzzled face of Mrs Swift appeared in the doorway, everything went misty and sparkling and the sparkles burst like stars and everybody shut their eyes, even Bouncer, and the neat little front room vanished as the walls fell away and the ceiling seemed to melt and the floor with its patterns of salt turned from red and brown and purple to a deep emerald green with tiny dark blue lines on it.

'Oh isn't it pretty?' said Elfrida.

And it was, for there was no sign of Acorn Lane or indeed of Queensam New Town. In fact the land had stopped being flat and had risen up into a series of low, rolling hills with a great wide river flowing placidly at their feet and on this side of the river there was the green grass and behind them was a forest full of the most extraordinary looking trees.

'I say,' said Roy, 'it's smashing, it really is ... hallo I can see you, Elfrida.'

'And I can see *you*,' said Elfrida, who was now as small and freckled as she had been in the time of Queen Elizabeth the First, although her long dress with its yellow embroidery looked more shabby than ever. Roy was wearing his T-shirt and jeans and Mr Patrick too was in his ordinary clothes, while as for Bouncer ...

'He's got his legs back,' shouted Roy, 'gosh how super, oh flip, GREAT!'

'Yap, howl, growl,' said Bouncer who anyway had never missed his one and a half legs.

'Congratulations,' said Roy, seizing hold of Mr

Patrick's hand and shaking it up and down. 'You've done everything right. Bouncer's all there and so is Elfrida and there's nothing more to worry about.'

'Nothing at all,' agreed Mr Patrick, 'apart from one or two small points such as *where* are we and *when* and *how* do we get out of here?'

'It doesn't matter where or when we are,' said Roy, hitching up his jeans and trying to make them more comfortable because they seemed to have shrunk recently, 'as long as we all get back, *visibly*, to our own time in Queensam. And then we can get Elfrida home and...'

'Oh yes,' said Mr Patrick, 'and how do we do all that, eh? My library books have vanished and so has the packet of salt!'

'Well,' Roy began and then stopped for the marshy ground on which they were all standing was going up and down, much as the springs of the sofa had done when Elfrida had bounced on them, and then there was a most peculiar snuffling and grunting sound which made everybody turn round and look in the direction of the strange forest. Branches and saplings stirred and waved about and then parted as the thud of hooves grew louder and then the edge of the forest seemed to bow down and a group of the most extraordinary looking animals came into view. They looked like a cross between a horse and an elephant with their great bulk and their arched necks and their long straight tusks. And behind them, although not in such great numbers, lumbered some creatures that were so weird looking that everybody,

Bouncer included, stared at them with their mouths wide open.

The Horse-Elephants (or Elephant-Horses) went galloping on until they reached the river bank where some of them then started to wash themselves down, throwing up their heads so that the water trickled down their strong straight tusks, splashing each other and churning up the mud, and generally making a great deal of noise and fuss; while a few of them moved a little way along the bank and drank and drank, throwing back their heads every now and then and shaking their thick necks.

Meanwhile the big creatures which had been lumbering along behind the Horse-Elephants shook their massive heads from side to side as they churned up the muddy ground and made for the water down-river. They were extremely large, and both Roy and Mr Patrick thought of the rhinoceros they had seen at the Zoo once upon a time but, although they were quite like those portly animals in build, these particular creatures were covered in long matted fur and had long thin noses.

'It *is* a dream,' muttered Mr Patrick. 'There aren't any animals like this. There can't ever have been...'

'They're real all right *now*,' said Roy. 'You can hear them, and feel them going past and you can jolly well smell them too!'

'I think they're ever so sweet,' said Elfrida, hitching up her skirt which was getting muddy. 'We get a lot of animals hanging round the castle in winter time you know because they get so hungry in the wild.

Wolves and deer, oxen and cats. I often go out and
feed them. Here, here, here...' and she snapped her
fingers.

'Don't *do* that,' said Roy, as some of the young
woolly rhinoceroses turned and looked enquiringly
in their direction. 'Don't you see, we're in the
Wrong Time and we mustn't make any sort of trouble,
because we'll never get back if we do.'

'It's not My Time,' Elfrida agreed, scratching behind the thick matted fleece of one of the young, if still
extremely large creatures which had sidled up to her
and was rubbing its enormous rump against a tree
trunk, while it smacked its tongue out of the corner
of its pink mouth. 'I've never seen creatures like this
before. What time is this?'

'It must be about half a million years ago—say
Hoxonian Interglacial,' replied Mr Patrick hoarsely.
'I think! Oh dear, oh goodness gracious me. Amazing,
astonishing, extraordinary. You do realise, of course,
that we've gone *far* too far back in history...'

'That was Bouncer's fault I suppose, wasn't it old
fellow?' said Elfrida, abandoning the woolly rhino
in order to pat Bouncer who in spite of having all
his legs restored didn't look at all happy as he turned
round and round with his mouth turned right down
at the corners.

'Yes it WAS,' agreed Mr Patrick, adding, 'Oh stop
that do, you silly creature,' as the young woolly rhino
butted him playfully in the stomach. 'Well, what do
we do now?'

Everybody turned and looked at Roy, even the

woolly rhino, which as its eyes were set very far apart because of the largeness of its face, meant that it had to keep swinging its head from side to side. Bouncer didn't care for the sight of that big, curved trunk bobbing about and he growled in the back of his throat and blew heavily through his white moustache.

'Shut up, the pair of you,' ordered Roy so fiercely that both animals obeyed him for at least a few seconds. 'Now look here,' Roy went on, jabbing one finger into Mr Patrick's brightly coloured shirt, 'first off, can't you remember the spell to get us back and secondly, does it have to be salt that you use? It was a firework last time, don't forget!'

'So it was,' agreed Mr Patrick brightening up. 'Anything white'll do really, I suppose. But I'm not an expert, I keep telling you.'

'You've done ever so well up till now,' put in Elfrida, who once again was scratching behind the ear of the woolly rhino which now had an expression of almost idiotic delight on its vast, and to be truthful, extremely ugly face.

'Oh, do you think so? You *are* kind, Princess Elfrida. Do tell me, in Your Time, this old Wickery that you keep referring to, was he a very powerful sort of magician?'

'No, not really. Chuck up chicken, don't lick Elfrida's sleeves, there's a lovey,' said Elfrida as the woolly rhino put out its enormous tongue and tried to wash her wrists. 'No, not really, Mr Patrick. He makes us all go out and gather herbs by the light of the full moon and then we boil them up, but I never see what good that does ... what's the matter Roy?'

'You are!' said Roy, who by this time was quite orange in the face with rage, 'here were are trapped half a million years out of our own time and with no idea of how we're going to get back to where we belong and yet all you can gab about is herbs and ... and ... old thingyme-bob and all the rest of it. Don't you realise that unless we do something jolly quickly we'll be STUCK HERE FOR EVER!'

Even as he spoke Roy had a sudden picture inside his mind of the History Teacher at Queensam Comprehensive saying something very similar to Roy's class, such as ...

'... can't you get it into your thick heads that unless you start TRYING to learn you might as well leave school *now*, because you're never going to get any further on in life EVER ...'

'It just shows,' said Roy Hatch, with his feet firmly planted in the thick rich mud of Middle Pleistocene Britain, 'that teachers are quite sensible sometimes. It's funny really.' Then he pulled himself together, gathering his wits as he did so because he knew that it was up to him and him alone to get this strangely assorted group back to safety as Mr Patrick, in spite of being a lot older in years than any of them, really had hardly any sense at all. But unfortunately it was already too late, for Bouncer had just made a playful nip at the thick forelock of the woolly rhino and that high spirited young animal immediately took exception and in hardly any time at all there was a wild scuffle of bodies, a couple of yelping roars, some howls and barks and before anybody had gathered their senses together Bouncer was off across the marshy flats as fast as he could go with the young woolly rhino thudding along behind and producing an excited howl as he did so.

All the other animals which had been bathing and drinking and generally enjoying the peaceful calm of the evening, stopped what they were doing and looked up enquiringly. It was hardly surprising as, of course, not one of them had ever seen a dog before.

'Bouncer,' shouted Roy and took off in pursuit.

'Roy,' said Elfrida, 'oh dear, oh dear,' and hitching up her awkwardly long skirt, off she went.

'Oh dear, oh dear, oh dear,' said Mr Patrick, 'never a *moment's* peace,' and he gave his spectacles a hasty polish, sighed and then began to run rather awkwardly after the others who by this time had reached the edge of the wide, slow-flowing river...

8. Woolly

As Bouncer, the young woolly rhino, Roy, Elfrida and as a very poor fifth, Mr Patrick, ran towards the river making a great deal of noise, all the animals stopped what they were doing, not because they were afraid, but because they were curious as to what on earth was happening. A giant beaver which had been stolidly gnawing at a vast tree trunk further up-stream, gave its front teeth a rest and blinked its little eyes in surprise before returning to its work. It could tell that autumn was close at hand and some deep instinct also told it that it was going to be the coldest autumn it had ever known. A cave bear, with its humped back and somewhat snouty face and short fat legs, put its head out of its front door on the opposite bank and yawned, before lumbering off awkwardly on its back paws to do a bit more hunting. While further downstream still, a cave lion blinked its yellow eyes as it came padding through the bushes. It was a great deal larger than any 20th century lion and it was just as well for Roy and Mr Patrick that they didn't catch sight of it.

However, the straight-tusked elephant-horses were by now turning this way and that and throwing back their heads and making uneasy yelping noises. They were the most nervous of the drinking and bathing creatures and it was one of them that suddenly let out a high shrill cry and began to stampede off down river. In a matter of seconds the rest of the herd had followed its example and there was a feeling of general panic and, as panic is extremely catching, the woolly rhinoceroses began behaving in the same silly way and in ten minutes flat Bouncer, the elderly mongrel from Queensam New Town, had succeeded in stampeding hundreds of prehistoric animals in all directions.

Nothing like it had occurred for at least the last half million years as the Hoxonian Interglacial (Mr Patrick had been perfectly correct) period was a very peaceful time and so it was Bouncer who was more or less responsible for making Kent such an interesting place for scientists in the future, as the skulls and bones of all kinds of fascinating animals were to be found in the new homes they had made for themselves far from this apparently noisy and dangerous river . . .

None of this of course entered the minds of Roy and Elfrida who had finally managed to corner Bouncer up against a mud bank as the young woolly rhino had got its long, curving tusk caught in a bright pink creeper with pretty white flowers. In spite of its prettiness the creeper was extremely tough, rather like plastic rubber, and it took the combined efforts of Mr Patrick and Elfrida to set the animal free. It stopped snorting and puffing and looked round for its mother, but she by now was a good three miles into South Kent and heading fast for the soft, green acres which a long, long way into the future would become the English Channel.

'Maaaa,' said the young woolly rhinoceros and attached itself to Elfrida, who stroked and smoothed it with one hand while with a tuft of rushes she tried to get the mud stains off her skirt with the other.

'You're a silly, SILLY dog,' Roy said to Bouncer, who promptly looked sadder than ever while he snorted through his moustache.

'Look here, Mr Patrick, WHITE flowers—couldn't

you get us back with them? Go on, do please try.'

'I don't feel at all well,' said Mr Patrick, and he had turned a rather nasty grey colour now that he was getting his breath back, 'but O.K. I'll have a go. Hang on a tick while I try and remember the words.'

Roy watched him extremely carefully, because he alone seemed to realise how full of peril their situation was. He would have been a great deal more scared if he had known that the cave lion, moving in circles, was getting closer and closer to them every second... As for Elfrida, she was perfectly happy to leave everything to Roy as she stroked first Bouncer and then Woolly, the young rhino.

The sun seemed to be going down very fast and a chill wind sprang up and began to rattle the leaves on the strange looking trees as Mr Patrick sank down on a tree stump, his head between his hands, as he tried to recall what he'd learnt about the Time Spell.

'All right,' he said suddenly, 'I think I've got it. Pick all the white flowers you can and then lay them out in the pattern that I tell you.'

Elfrida and Roy did as they were asked, but as it was growing darker by the half minute it became quite difficult to follow Mr Patrick's instructions and he kept on asking for another flower and another and still another. And all the time the cave lion was padding in closer and closer with its eyes gleaming as yellow as the sun had been, while it sniffed and sniffed and licked its jaws.

'Yes, yes, that's it ... I think,' said Mr Patrick, straining his short-sighted eyes in the gloom.

'But that's the shape of my castle,' said Elfrida, bending forward.

'And the tracks I made with my bike on Queensam Keep,' put in Roy. 'It's like the pattern we saw from the top of the Tower, isn't it?'

'Grrrrrr,' muttered the cave lion which by this time was very close indeed. Both Bouncer, who had been dozing off in the nice soft mud, and young Woolly heard it, and their ears went back and the pair of them stopped being enemies and became friends in the face of what they instinctively realised must be a common foe. So Bouncer glanced at the rhino and let his white fur lie down flat and young Woolly stopped butting his horn this way and the other and they moved closer together. Nobody else noticed and Mr Patrick started to mutter under his breath and Elfrida reached out and grasped Roy's cold hand and Roy gripped hers tightly and Mr Patrick's voice grew louder and louder and quite suddenly the last of the pale sunlight seemed to vanish and the cold became so bad that everybody moved closer together.

'The glaciers are coming,' said Mr Patrick. 'Another ice age ...'

And then his words were swallowed up by a rushing noise and Roy, who was the only one who had his eyes open, saw an enormous lion with yellow eyes preparing to spring on them, while high above and beyond it there seemed to be great mountains of ice and snow of quite unbelievable cold, so he very sensibly shut his eyes too and there was that now familiar sick and giddy sensation as though he was being churned round and round in a washing machine . . .

There was a long silence, and then Mr Patrick said shakily, 'Well, we're back, I *think* . . .'

And they were, only they had moved from Mrs Swift's front parlour to quite a different part of Queensam and what was more . . .

'We've brought it with us!' said Roy.

And they had! For there, looking rather dazed was the young woolly rhino with Bouncer yawning and scratching himself against the animal's sturdy fetlocks. But there was no sign of Elfrida at all.

'I don't feel at all well,' said Mr Patrick again, 'and anyway, where are we?'

'Some sort of building site,' said Roy, getting his own breath back and wishing that his stomach would settle down and stop rocking about. 'Elfrida, are you there?'

'Yes,' said a small miserable voice in the dusk. 'I'm here, but I'm invisible again, aren't I? Oh brother, oh flip!'

'Never mind,' said Roy, giving her small unseen hand a hard shake before letting it go, 'that spell Old Wickery put on you must be stronger than you realised, but we will break it in the end, you'll see.'

'Yes when I'm about a hundred and ten,' Elfrida replied grumpily. Roy was about to point out that in a way she was already a great deal older than even

THAT, when fortunately Woolly, slowly coming out
of his state of shock, stepped backwards and called
loudly for his mother. The cry of a young Middle-
Pleistocene animal is rather eerie at the best of
times, in the middle of a building site in Queensam
New Town it was really quite extraordinary, and it
certainly made everybody forget their own immedi-
ate troubles.

'Hush, hush, hush,' said Elfrida, starting to stroke
his thick woolly hide.

'Get the beast off my foot!' yelled Mr Patrick,
pushing at the animal's large and solid rump with all
his strength.

'Shhhhh, everybody,' said Roy.

Bouncer yawned, spreadeagled himself in the mud
in his favourite position and dropped off to sleep.
He'd had a long, tiring day for a dog of his age.

'I expect it's hungry,' said Elfrida. 'I know *I* am.
I wonder what animals like this eat?'

Roy searched through his pockets and found a con-
gealing bag of toffees and offered those on the flat
of his hand. Woolly sniffed at them and then, with
one lick of his enormous pink tongue, took the lot
and started to munch, paper-bag and all. It was an
unwittingly good move on Roy's part as the toffees
quite soon became so sticky that the animal couldn't
have made any more noise if it had wanted to. It also
obligingly removed its great foot from Mr Patrick's
and chewed and chewed, blinking its little eyes,
while it leant fondly against Elfrida who was still
tickling it behind its ears.

'I think all my toes must be broken,' said Mr Patrick, slipping off his shoe and massaging away. 'Well, *now* what?'

Roy, who had been having a closer look at their surroundings, made up his mind in a way which he would never have been able to do a short while ago, but then he had never before had people (one of them grown up) and animals depending on him like this, and he said loudly and clearly,

'First, we find somewhere to tie up this—this animal. Secondly you go home Mr Patrick and—and make up some story if Mrs Swift is upset or anything...'

'She will be! What story?'

'That,' said Roy fiercely into the gloom at Mr Patrick's pale face, 'is up to you. Thirdly, Elfrida and I go back home.'

'And get something to eat?' asked Elfrida hopefully.

'Yes, O.K. And fourthly, I take Bouncer back to Mr Cliff. At least Bouncer's all right again because his legs are all there. And fifthly we meet tomorrow to decide what to do next. O.K.?'

To Roy's secret surprise everybody agreed to this plan and within a very short while young Woolly, still chewing on the toffees, had been firmly secured to a bulldozer, Mr Patrick, muttering and talking to himself, had gone padding away to make his peace with Mrs Swift and Roy had stopped off at the Chinese Restaurant to buy some take-away fish and chips for Elfrida. He left her in the shadows and eating away as fast as she could go while he returned Bouncer to Mr Cliff.

'Well he looks a bit done in,' said Mr Cliff, blowing through his white moustache as he spoke. 'Had a lot of exercise, old chap?'

'Yes he *has*,' said Roy, thinking of the stampeding of the straight-tusked elephant-horses, not to mention the flight of all the prehistoric animals and the sudden appearance of that gigantic lion...

'Not as young as he was,' said Mr Cliff, shaking his head, 'like the rest of us. Funny thing though Roy, you remember me telling you about a niece of ours who died. Mmm? Well, we had a letter today from overseas, something about her having a daughter. We've never heard of any family before now and we can't make head nor tail of it at all. Mrs Cliff's all of a state, quite cheered her up it has. Funny, isn't it? Come on Bouncer, old chap.'

Granny Hatch looked over her spectacles and said, 'Ah *there* you are! Now look you, Roy, what have you been up to, eh? There's Mrs Swift been round to see me and in an awful state too, saying that she'd seen you at her place with her lodger, he's the Children's Librarian at the library, and that one moment there you were in her front parlour and the next moment there you were not at all. I told her she must have dozed off and dreamt it. Seems a funny sort of dream though, doesn't it?'

'I don't know, Gran,' muttered Roy, who felt (and quite rightly) that he'd been through enough for one day, 'but I really am ever so hungry. Could I have *two* Welsh rarebits please?'

'Oh very well, I suppose it's all the growing that you're doing that makes you so hungry. But I'll tell you this, Roy, there's something odd going on in the Town and I suspect,' and Granny Hatch looked over and then under her spectacles in a frightening way, 'that you know more about it than you're telling!'

Roy didn't say anything at all in reply, but he had a creepy sort of feeling that his Granny was checking up on him and he said so to Elfrida when he got the second Welsh rarebit, by this time rather cold and stringy, up to the attic.

'What CAN she know?' asked Elfrida, digging her invisible teeth into the soggy toast. 'Is there anything for afters?'

Roy handed over two packets of crisps, some salted biscuits and a yoghurt and returned to his bedroom, where, in spite of being very tired indeed, he had all kinds of nightmares about the young woolly rhino, his Granny, Mr Patrick and Elfrida. So it was quite a relief to wake up, although what he seemed to be hearing through his dreams was a high pitched and then a low pitched wail which was a bit like the cry of Woolly, and then Roy shot up out of his bed as he realised that what he was really hearing was the rise and fall of a police car siren.

'Oh flip,' said Roy, throwing back the bed-clothes. 'They've found HIM.' And he made a dive for his shirt and jeans.

9. Sanctuary

It was so early that everything was still rather shadowy and Roy was going carefully, so as to get his bike out without making a noise, when there was a soft patter of footsteps and Elfrida said breathlessly, 'What is it?

What's happening?'

'Don't know, but I'll bet it's something to do with Woolly getting discovered. I'd better go and see anyway.'

'I'm coming too. If he's in trouble then I want to be there to help him. I think he's lovely.'

As Woolly was about the ugliest animal that Roy had ever seen, this was a surprising remark, but then he remembered a hideous old grey rat with bitten ears of which he had been extremely fond when he was young, so he nodded and grunted and held the bike steady while Elfrida climbed up into the saddle and then Roy gave it a push and swung his right leg over the handlebars and began to pedal as hard as he could go. In spite of being small Elfrida was no light weight and as it was so early and this was a matter of some urgency, Roy decided to take a chance and to ride across Queensam Park. He was about a third of the way across the grass when Elfrida buzzed in his ear.

'Look out—the castle walls.'

'But they're not *there*.'

'Well, I think they will be if *I'm* with you. Better safe than sorry anyway. Turn left and keep straight on for a bit. Remember what happened last time.'

It was probably lucky for Elfrida that Roy needed all his breath for cycling as he might have replied to this remark with some bitterness. After all, the 'last time' had resulted in a chain of events in which disaster had followed on disaster, what with Bouncer losing one and a half legs for a bit, Mr Patrick getting stranger and stranger, people nearly being put in prison and people being hunted by a gigantic lion, let alone almost being trapped half a million years before their time. But what really rankled was the fact that not only was Elfrida still invisible, but most of Roy's careful savings were rapidly going the same way because she cost such a lot to feed, but how would a Royal Princess ever understand a person being broke?

'Turn right.'

'WAA-WAA-WAA-WAA...'

A police car hurtled down the road a hundred yards ahead of them and then its tyres squealed as it rounded a curve and above all this noise Roy and Elfrida heard an all too familiar trumpeting.

'Look here,' said Roy, putting on the brakes as they sped off the grass, 'what are we going to do about old Woolly? How *can* we help him?'

'You can't, I can,' said Elfrida briskly. 'He's my friend and I'll try and rescue him just like you did me. O.K.?'

'O.K.,' said Roy, going rather red about the neck, because he'd come very close to grumbling to Elfrida as to all the trouble she'd caused and now, in a sort of way, she made him feel a bit ashamed. 'But what'll you *do*?'

'Well, I think I'll have a go at riding him, it won't be any more bumpy than being on your bike-cycle.'

'BI-cycle.'

'Yes. And I'm quite good at pony riding actually, even the Head Cook said so. And, with any luck,

I'll be able to get Woolly to a cave that's not very far from here.'

'I jolly well bet it's not there *now*.'

'Oh, I don't suppose caves vanish all that easily. I mean I don't see how they could really, and then I'll get a lift back to you—being invisible does have a few good things about it—in time for breakfast. I'm EVER SO . . .'

'Hungry, *I* know. All right, but do be careful, I don't suppose Woolly's ever been ridden in his life. No, he can't have been . . .' said Roy stopping dead, 'because I don't think there *were* people in the world all that time ago. I say, Elfrida . . .'

'Oh hush,' replied Elfrida who was in a very bossy mood this morning, as there's nothing like a good night's sleep and the call of a friend in trouble to make you feel braver than usual, 'I can hear . . . oh goodness, oh what a din . . . all sorts of noises and people talking. People in Your Time talk much more *at* each other than we do in Ours. Yes, yes I can hear Woolly and he's ever so upset, poor lamb . . .'

'Hardly a lamb, more like a rhinoceros.'

'Shhhh . . . oh dear. I'll get off here, thank you Roy.'

'I say, Elfrida a . . .'

But the bicycle had already grown lighter and then there was that soft tap of running footsteps which quite quickly vanished as the WAAA-WAAA of the police car and the trumpeting of poor Woolly filled the normally peaceful air of Queensam.

As Roy sat still on his bicycle, Elfrida, her long

skirt caught up and wrapped round her girdle in
folds so that she could run easily, tuned her sharp
ears into the cause of all the trouble. It wasn't difficult at all for her to slide past the police car which
had come to a halt and now had a flashing blue light
going round and round on its roof.

Apart from three somewhat worried looking young
policemen, who were all standing very close to their
car, there were two other vehicles drawn up on the
lay-by near the building site. One was a moped and
the other was a somewhat elderly saloon car and,
apart from the voices which were coming over the
radio in the police car, two other voices were raised
in a high pitched argument. The older and much
crosser voice was saying.

'I've had just about enough of you, young fellow.
You and your jokes! All this Flower Power and
Hippy malarky! Well, we don't need it in Queensam
let me tell you ...'

'But all that Flower Power stuff was ages ago and
anyway, Mr Wickens ...'

'Oh yes, *I* see, trying to make me feel even more
out of date, are you? Well, it won't work! I've
already had a word with the Borough Librarian
and he's having a word with the County Librarian
and speaking as a Councillor who's on the Library
Committee I can truthfully say that your career
here is over! Are you listening ...?'

'Of course I'm listening,' said Mr Patrick, sounding
unusually firm for him, 'I haven't got much choice,
have I? What with you shouting the way you are.

All I'm trying to tell you, you silly old man.. '

'WHAT DID YOU CALL ME?'

'Yelp, yelp, yelp,' said Woolly, putting back his ugly head and making as much noise as he could, as he slowly came into view round the bulldozer.

As Woolly had a very loud voice (both the toffees and the bag had long ago disappeared and like Elfrida he was very aware of having an empty stomach) the din was considerable. Added to which the sight of a young woolly rhino, which, give or take a century or two, was about half a million years out of date, was so unusual that all three policemen stepped back, paused, took another look at Woolly's enormous gaping mouth and then as though pulled by invisible strings made a dash into their patrol car. Three doors slammed simultaneously and three windows were closed. It was to Mr Wickens' great credit that he didn't make a dive for his own car instead he looked over the top of his spectacles, shook his head in plain disbelief and then jabbing Mr Patrick in the chest with a finger he said, 'I am NOT a silly old man, and I don't know what kind of a zoo you've hi-jacked that animal from, but you'll take it back there right away. I don't think it's at all funny playing about with Council property in this manner, and if that hippo or rhino or whatever it is, has done any damage you'll pay for it! Understood?'

'It is not...' began Mr Patrick, practically jumping up and down in his agitation, 'It is NOT a joke. This is an actual prehistoric ... oh ...'

'Shut up,' hissed Elfrida, in Mr Patrick's ear. 'He'll only think you've gone mad or something. He's ever so like Old Wickery, *he* doesn't like people playing jokes either. Actually he's ever so like Old Wickery a lot of the time. Just don't argue and I'll get Woolly away. O.K.?'

Woolly, who alone of those present appeared to be able to see Elfrida, turned and looked towards her and put down his head as she scratched him behind one ear and then, hitching up her skirts again, Elfrida made a scrambling jump for his back and once she had got into a more or less comfortable position she gripped hold of his tangled mane and kicked with her heels and Woolly gave a snort and started to jog trot straight towards Mr Wickens who nimbly stepped out of his path.

Woolly put back his head and gave another yelping cry and within seconds and before anybody had got their breath back he had awkwardly cantered off into the mist and disappeared. There was a long, long silence during which nobody spoke, although there was a steady criss-cross of voices on the radio of the police car and then Mr Wickens said slowly,

'Right, that's it! I don't know how you managed your conjuring tricks, young man, nor do I know why you've done 'em, seeing that you had a good job in this town. Anything for a laugh I suppose! You Young People Today have got No Sense of Responsibility. However, and be that as it may, you won't work in Queensam any more. I can't sack you, more's the pity, but when the Library Committee meets I'll make quite certain that we've no place for you in this town. Nor in this part of the country, neither.'

Roy, who under cover of the mist had managed to scramble quite close, heard these awful words and didn't know what to do. Should he jump up and try and explain everything? Or would that only make everything worse? And, in any case, where should he begin to start explaining the whole tangled adventure?

It was Mr Patrick who solved the whole situation. He drew himself up and put back his shoulders and stuck out his chin and quite suddenly he seemed to look a great deal taller and less pale than usual as he said quietly, 'It wasn't a joke, Mr Wickens. I thought I heard the cry of—of someone in distress and I came to find out if I was needed. Apparently I wasn't. I formally resign from the library immediately. I'm sorry that you have been troubled.'

And Mr Patrick bowed his head in a sharp jerky manner and then walked over to his moped, kicked the starter and with a gentle phut-phut-phut, he too vanished down the road before anybody made a move to try and stop him.

'Impudent young know-all,' muttered Mr Wickens and pulling down his jacket he went over to the police car while Roy slid backwards and made for his bike as fast as he could with his brain going round and round in circles. He'd got even more problems to deal with now! Mr Patrick had just lost his job, while as for Elfrida, there she was galloping off towards the Motorway on Woolly's back looking for a probably non-existent cave.

'Oh help,' muttered Roy as he made a flying start on his bike and set off in pursuit of Elfrida and Woolly, 'what next . . . ?'

He hadn't covered more than a hundred yards when there was a phut-phut-phut and Mr Patrick, sitting very upright on his moped, came into view and flagged Roy down.

'Never catch her on that,' he said, nodding at the bike. 'I'll give you a lift.'

'No thanks. And I bet I *will* catch them, because Woolly's too heavy to keep up much of a speed for long *and* he'll be bouncing Elfrida about like anything. She'll try and slow him down.'

'Good thinking,' said Mr Patrick, who like Elfrida was suddenly being alarmingly brisk. 'Come on then, before Old Wickens and his Police pals set off in pursuit too. They will, you know, any minute now! At least Woolly's easy to track.'

And indeed he was, for his enormous feet had picked up a great deal of powdered cement and mud and the prints left by a trotting Woolly Rhinoceros are quite unmistakable and, of course, in this particular case they were unique.

It was very lucky for both Elfrida and her allies that it was so early in the morning because it meant that there wasn't much traffic about. Elfrida had started off full of confidence, because in her Own Time she knew this part of Kent extremely well as she had often criss-crossed it by foot and on ponyback while looking for old Roman vineyards, fruit bushes and trees and, at this time of year particularly, mushrooms. Late summer has a smell that is very much its own, a kind of mixture of bonfire smoke and wet fallen leaves and general mistiness. Elfrida sniffed it deeply and for a moment or two she almost felt home —or rather castle—sick and then she remembered a lot of other things about her old life and she suddenly realised with a shiver right up the whole length of her back, that visible or invisible, she didn't really want to go back to it after all ...

This new world was dreadfully noisy and confusing and full of all kinds of strange ideas like people not talking to each other very much and being ordered to do this and that, or *not* to do that and this, but then there were a lot of nice things too ... hot water which came straight out of the wall, bartering places where you could get a new dress (every year probably) and lots and lots and lots of absolutely delicious food which people like Granny Hatch kept in a great big cold chest.

It was as though Elfrida's thoughts about food had travelled directly to Woolly, who suddenly slowed his ponderous jog-trot and put back his head and bellowed out the news that his stomach was empty, and that sticky toffees were no meal for a growing rhino.

'Shhh,' said Elfrida. 'Hold on a tick, Woolly, while I work out where we are.... Now there should be a

rise in the forest over there ... oh bother, all the
trees have gone. You know, it's very difficult to work
out *what* should be *where* when all the tracks have
been changed and places have been knocked down. I
mean there ought to be a Roman Big House somewhere to the left and then a river and a vineyard
with criss-cross streams and a high bank past that
with a cave in it. I think ... only it's all different
now.'

It was indeed, for Elfrida and Woolly were now on
the approach lane to the M-Road which slices through
this part of Kent and although it is banked up every
so often there are certainly no signs left of Roman
villas, orchards and vineyards.

'Oh well, it—the cave you know—must be here
somewhere,' said Elfrida and kicked Woolly in the
flanks. He obediently lumbered forward again and so
Elfrida-of-the-Castle and a young Woolly Rhinoceros took to the Motorway.

Strangely enough it made the job of their friendly
pursuers much easier for, ignoring the notice which
forbade motor bikes under a certain c.c., let alone
pedal bikes, both Roy and Mr Patrick learnt to read
the signs of Elfrida's and Woolly's progress quite
quickly. All they had to do was to keep their eyes
skinned for an occasional motorist or lorry driver
who had come to a halt on the soft shoulder and who
had their heads buried in their hands.

'There they are!' shouted Mr Patrick as Woolly's
lumbering shape came into view through the mist.

'Elfrida, get off the Motorway,' implored Roy,

standing on his pedals as he followed close behind Mr Patrick.

And quite suddenly Elfrida did exactly that as she at last recognised a familiar landmark and digging her heels into Woolly's by now heaving flanks she got him to cross the on-coming traffic. (It was very lucky for all of them that the Motorway was so empty), and Roy and Mr Patrick, were so intent on following Woolly that they had long ago forgotten their highway code and did the same. The police car which was still some way behind them, didn't see what was happening and went whaa-whaa on its way into the mist.

'You see!' said Elfrida some little while later, 'The cave *is* still here. I always thought it would be, you know,' and she crossed her fingers behind her back as she spoke.

'Goodness,' said Mr Patrick, letting his moped fall over with a crash, 'but it's smashing, astonishing. It really is. Oh what a vault of treasure. Elfrida, how did you know what route to follow? It's absolutely fantastic...'

Everybody, even Woolly, turned round and round and looked about them at the great cavern whose entrance until now had been disguised by the brambles, trees and shrubs which had grown across it.

At one end there was what appeared to be a kind of throne and before it a long, curved stone table. There was something very grand and majestic about this enormous cave which even Woolly appeared to feel as he stopped panting and complaining about his empty stomach.

'It's *his* place,' said the voice of Elfrida. 'He always told us that if we were threatened we could come here and be safe and He would save us. The difficulty always was to find it.'

'Who,' said Mr Patrick, his voice echoing off the great vaulted roof of the cave. '*Who* told you that, Elfrida?'

Elfrida slid off the heaving back of Woolly and in that moment, invisible or not, she was a Princess.

'The Great General From The West,' she said, her voice going on and on and on round the cave.

Roy looked dumbly at Mr Patrick who was slowly sinking down on one knee, while he took off his crash helmet and put it under one arm and bowed his head, as he said, 'Now I understand. The Great General From The West. The One who was going to save us all from all dangers ... from invaders and from darkness. Only now we call him King Arthur.'

'Yes,' said Elfrida from the shadows, 'that's right, King Arthur.'

10. *The Third Spell*

It was very quiet in the big cave, so quiet that you could hear Woolly breathing in and out through his mouth and the rumble of his enormous stomach. So quiet that Roy could hear the steadily growing roar and hum of the traffic on the Motorway which kept reminding him that if he didn't get a move on he'd be late with his paper round and then there'd be trouble and how could he possibly ever explain all this to Granny? Roy shifted round on his bike and then shrugged and decided that there wasn't very much he could do in any case, as Mr Patrick looked as if he'd gone into a sort of trance, while there had been no sound at all from Elfrida for at least ten minutes.

On the Motorway the police car drew over to the left with its blue light whirling round and round and Mr Wickens in his car came to a halt behind it. Everybody got out and compared notes.

'We've lost him,' said Mr Wickens, 'lost all of 'em. Now tell me, Constable, what have you got written down in that notebook of yours, eh?'

It was the same young policeman who had caught Roy and the others earlier on and he shifted about a bit before reading out his notes. It really did sound rather ridiculous in the increasing light of day to say that he had suddenly out of nowhere seen people appear on a traffic island, but he read out aloud steadily as his face got pinker and pinker.

'All right, all right,' said Mr Wickens, 'and I've seen a thing or two as well that'd take a lot of explaining and as for you lads, what have you got to say for yourselves?'

The other two policemen in the patrol car hadn't had the time to compare notes so that their reports were even more muddled and uncertain. At the finish all three of them looked at each other and then at Councillor Wickens. It seemed that there had been some trespassing, that some Council property might have been damaged, that a noise had been made and that possibly a circus animal had been captured and attached if rather inadequately, to Council property. This same circus animal had since disappeared and had not yet been resighted, let alone recaptured.

'It was,' said the youngest policeman, 'a very strange sort of creature, not the sort of which I've ever seen before.'

The other two policemen nodded and shuffled their feet.

Councillor Wickens drew in his breath and said sharply,

'Very well, lads, I'll see your Sergeant later. Meanwhile I intend to carry on my own private enquiries as I'm not satisfied at all as to what's been going on in Queensam. There's been a funny feeling all round the town of late. Unrest I'd call it, and what's more I'd lay the cause of it all at the feet of ... but never mind that. Well I'm off.'

The policemen saluted smartly and then quickly climbed back into their car and, once they had got up a bit of speed, the young constable said, 'I'll tell you what, it's like as the Councillor said. My wife, Jenny she was down in the shopping area the other day getting this and that, and when I came home that evening she said as how nobody ever spoke to anybody in the town. She'd had a bit of a chat with a young boy, nothing much it was, but she said it was about the first time that she'd spoken to anybody in the neighbourhood. Well, that can't be right can it? I mean it's not natural, is it? We all go about here as if we're invisible or something...'

'I'm not saying you're right nor wrong,' agreed the policeman who was driving the car, 'only it's funny you should mention that. My wife, she says the same. She goes into town to do the shopping like and nobody speaks to anybody so she says. In fact...' and he lowered his voice, 'she did say, and she's Kentish born being of an Appledore family, that it's like this part of the County is...' and he stopped suddenly.

'Is what?' asked the second young policeman.

'Never you mind,' was the answer and there was a long pause and then the driver said in a low voice, 'It's not as it should be. Well then, if you must ask, there's a sort of bad wishing on it. Don't dare laugh nor snigger, P.C. Swift!'

'I'm not doing anything of the sort,' said P.C. Swift, 'by crikey I'm not, 'cause my Aunty Swift she's said the same many a time. She says as Queensam has got something bad on it that was put there long ago ... she even blames her rheumatism on it.'

The panda car gathered speed and vanished into the mist and at exactly the same moment in the cave Mr Patrick said, 'Someone's coming, but it's not ...'

A car drew up somewhere and there was the sound of hurried footsteps and in the doorway appeared the fat, angry figure of Mr Wickens.

'So I've found you,' he said, 'I guessed you were mixed up in this business somewhere! Now what have you got to say for yourselves?'

Everybody bunched together, even Woolly, as they stared at him. He was blocking out a lot of the daylight and his shadow looked enormous as it stretched out in front of him, while as the sun grew stronger the mist curled and twisted like smoke from a fire all round him.

Elfrida forgot she was invisible and therefore safe and let out a yelp of fright.

'It's Old Wickery, it is, it is, he's come to get me again to lock me up. Oh, oh, OH!' And she buried her head in Woolly's matted, somewhat smelly, but very reassuringly solid flank.

'That's what they used to call me at school when I was a lad,' said Mr Wickens, forgetting to be angry for a moment. 'I haven't heard that nickname in thirty-five years. Here—who was speaking then?'

'It was,' gabbled Roy, desperately trying to think of a way out of this new unforeseen danger, 'it was something to do with the echoes I expect. How did *you* find *us*?'

'It wasn't difficult following that beast's tracks and the moment I saw where they were leading I suddenly seemed to remember ... here I think I'll sit down for a moment. I don't feel too good.'

Mr Patrick, who having found Elfrida's invisible shoulder, had been patting it and telling her in a low voice not to worry as nobody was going to hurt her, took a look at Mr Wickens' face, which even though it was in shadow, appeared to have turned a sickly lead colour, and with two strides he crossed over to him and with no ceremony at all, sat him down on a rock and pushed his head down on to his knees.

Roy, Elfrida and Woolly continued to stare in a sort of trance-like way at what was going on and Roy had a curious feeling that he could hear Time rushing past like a great wind.

'Better?' asked Mr Patrick, his voice echoing.

'A bit thanks.' Mr Wickens raised his head and wiped his forehead with the back of his hand. 'It was the shock, I suppose. Seeing that great animal ...' He glanced uneasily at Woolly who was yawning hugely, 'and hearing voices out of the past and suddenly remembering this place. I used to come here often as a lad, I used to make up fanciful stories about it to do with knights and dragons and all that stuff, and then I forgot about it. It went clean out of my mind for nearly forty years until just five minutes ago. It's given me a jolt, it really has. The mind can play us some funny tricks. Pardon me, I'll be fit in a minute or two.'

And Mr Wickens, as though hypnotised by Woolly's gaping jaws, yawned almost as widely himself and then leant his head back against the wall of the cave, breathing deeply as he closed his eyes.

'It's shock, all right,' whispered Mr Patrick moving softly over to Roy, 'I've seen people behave like this after an accident. It's fascinating isn't it? The cave became invisible to him as soon as he started to grow up, I suppose. Perhaps only young people can ever find it, and of course they'd never tell because it would be their secret place.'

'You're not young,' said Elfrida, who'd had quite a shock herself, 'I mean, you're a grown-up person.'

'Not in my mind,' said Mr Patrick, staring fiercely at the chalk walls, 'at the Home they used to call me a Late Developer, but it wasn't really that at all. I just didn't want to belong to the grown-up world. And I never have and I never will. There are quite a lot of people like that, you know; we just don't seem to fit in somehow. But that's not the point at the moment. The point IS that we've got to get Woolly out of Our Time, because if we leave him here his life'll be a misery. There'll be scientists and doctors and vets and goodness knows who else pushing and prodding him. They might even put him to sleep and carve him...'

'No, no,' wailed Elfrida, 'I won't let them. I won't!'

'You wouldn't be able to stop 'em,' said Roy, who like Mr Patrick was now staring at the wall. 'I say Mr Patrick, it's chalk ... white ... could it work?'

'It just might. Worth a try anyway and we'd better shift ... listen.'

The all too recognisable whaa-whaa whaa-whaa was growing louder on the Motorway and although it was possible that the panda car was not looking for them at all, everybody was by now feeling so thoroughly guilty about the kidnapping of Woolly that Mr Patrick, Roy and Elfrida began picking up pieces of chalk rubble as fast as they could.

Mr Patrick drew the now familiar pattern with great care, murmuring under his breath as he did so and making absolutely certain that he kept well clear of Mr Wickens who was now snoring steadily. He also drew so that the grumbling Woolly was well inside the pattern and then when he had finished, just to make extra certain-sure, Mr Patrick made everybody bunch together.

'I'll tell you why,' he said in answer to Roy's enquiring look. 'It's because every time we've gone on a journey—there or back—something's gone wrong like Bouncer losing one-and-a-half legs.'

'Well, nothing can go wrong *this* time,' said Roy, who had his back to Mr Wickens by the door, so he didn't notice the way in which a stiffening breeze was blowing across the chalk lines and making them blurr and shift closer and closer to Mr Wickens' large feet...

'I do wish you knew your proper Time, Elfrida,' said Mr Patrick, 'it'd make things *so* much easier. Well, we fell short with the first spell and we overstepped the Date Line far too much with the second, still with you knowing about the General I can only suppose ... well here we go. Hold tight.'

As Mr Patrick spoke the whaaa-whaaa whaaa-whaaa and the rumble of the traffic rose up in a great tidal wave of sound which seemed to be about to topple over on top of them, and then it faded and grew less and less as everything whirled round and round with a rushing hiss which also fell away until it was so quiet that Roy could hear the rumble of Woolly's empty stomach.

Slowly Roy opened his eyes and looked about and then he looked again, turning his head as far as he could and staring up and then down.

'It's O.K.,' he said grumpily, letting go of Mr Patrick's hand and then Elfrida's, 'you can stop crouching like a couple of owls, because nothing's happened. We're still HERE. It just hasn't worked this time. It's gone wrong.'

Mr Patrick opened his eyes, looked about and sighed deeply and Elfrida did the same, but a fraction of a second later she gave Roy a great push that sent him toppling against Woolly as she shouted,

'No, it hasn't. I'M HERE. I'm not invisible. I can see my hands and my arms and my skirt and my feet and there's the end of my plait—goodness my hair needs washing again—and anyway the cave *isn't* the same because it hasn't got any bushes and brambles across the door and ... OH! WHAT'S THAT?'

'That' was a shadowy sort of shape which was sitting, or at least half sitting and half standing by the door. It was a kind of See-Through version of Mr Wickens and there was a slight pause while everybody stared at him, and then Woolly gave a high pitched bellow and thundered out of the cave with a thud thud thud which made everybody's teeth judder in their heads.

Roy reacted first and just managed to grab the end of Woolly's thick tail, Elfrida caught hold of Roy's jacket, Mr Patrick got the end of Elfrida' flying plait and the Misty-Mr-Wickens came tumbling after all of them, and then in his half-invisible way bounced back as everybody had come to a standstill.

They certainly *had* moved for the Motorway and all its traffic had vanished completely, and before them lay rolling grassland which dipped down to a shallow valley that was bordered on both sides by what had once been vineyards, and there was still some rather overgrown evidence of a very grand Roman villa. The columns and the courtyard were covered with creeping ivy and vines and the shallow steps which once upon a time had lead to the central section of the villa had cracked and become very uneven.

'There!' said Elfrida, 'I remember! We pick grapes from those vines still, *and* collect the tiles to stand our hot cooking pots on.'

'That's vandalism,' said Mr Patrick angrily.

'No, no, NO,' contradicted Elfrida, 'WE'RE not the Vandals. THEY come from the North-East, you know, in their Long Boats. That's what we're always told and if you don't keep quiet in the scullery-maid's dormitory after candles-out, THEY come and take you to be a slave and then you have to work in a kitchen for ever and ever, and THEY never give you enough to eat...'

Elfrida's voice tailed into silence as she realised that everybody was looking at her in a surprised sort of way. Her upper lip grew longer and longer and her face started to crumble and then she gave a kind of howl and pushed her hands up against her eyes as she fell on to her knees, rocking backwards and forwards.

Mr Patrick and Roy looked at each other and both of them would have given practically anything at all to have been somewhere else at this particular moment, because seeing somebody else being very unhappy is not at all a comfortable feeling for the person looking on.

'I'm not a Princess,' wailed Elfrida, 'I'm not. I just pretended, because I always wanted to be one. I'm, I'm ...' and she caught her breath, 'I just work in the kitchens of the castle, that's all ...'

Mr Patrick took a step forward and knelt down on one knee with his crash helmet under his arm.

'It doesn't matter what sort of job you've got,' he said hoarsely, 'because you're a Princess to me. May I be your Knight?'

Roy gathered his wits together and following Mr Patrick's lead, he said,

'And I will be your—your ...' he looked sideways desperately and at the same moment from somewhere he remembered something he had once read at school and added, 'I will be your Squire, Princess Elfrida.'

And like Mr Patrick, Roy fell on one knee and bowed his head before Elfrida-the-Scullery-Maid-Princess.

'Oh dear, oh goodness, oh thank you,' said Elfrida wiping the back of one dusty hand across her face. 'It's ever so kind of you and I—er—accept your offers. Thank you. Rise Sir Patrick, Rise Squire Roy.'

And she tapped the pair of them on the shoulder with a convenient stick. Mr Patrick did think of pointing out that really his name should be 'Sir Hugh' but it seemed slightly bad mannered under the circumstances, so he winked at Roy, polished his spectacles on the seat of his tattered jeans and taking away the 'dubbing' stick, he led the way down the path.

'You see,' said Elfrida, skipping along beside Roy and clutching on to Woolly's tail. 'You see, I knew you'd find out in the end, but it's only a game really, pretending to be a Princess. You don't mind do you?'

'No, it's a bit of a relief actually. NOW you can pay for your own ice-creams and fish and chips, because you're an ordinary person like me. I don't think Royal people *do* pay for stuff like chips and bus fares. They're always being treated by Mayors and things. At least they are when they come to Queensam. Oh!'

'Yes,' said Elfrida nodding rather sadly, 'I'm back where I belong now in my Own Time and I'm visible, *but* . . .' and her bottom lip trembled, 'but I'd ever so much rather be visible in Your Time. WE don't have chips, or ices or everlasting hot water or bike-cycles.'

'BI-cycles.'

'That's right. And then there's Bouncer, oh I *shall* miss him, and your Granny who does all that lovely cooking, and television and bartering places.'

'Shops . . .'

'Yes, and going to school.'

'You CAN'T WANT TO GO TO SCHOOL,' said Roy, appalled.

'Yes I do. Because I jolly well bet *you* don't get no food if you haven't learnt your spells right...'

'No we don't. Because we don't learn spells for a start off and...'

'And you can ride in lifts-and-lowers and...'

'Hold on,' said Roy loudly and he caught hold of Elfrida's arms. He then crossed his own arms and looked at her so sternly that everybody, even the see-through Mr Wickens, came to a halt and looked at him. And the strange thing was that in the early autumn sunlight, with the shadows dappling across his face, and with his feet apart and firmly planted and his shoulders squared, Roy seemed to be the sort of person who you *would* stop and listen to.

'Hold on,' Roy repeated. 'You, Elfrida, were the one who was always going on and on about everybody looking cross, or not speaking in Queensam. You complained all the time! You were always saying how much better your Own Time was. Oh yes you were,' as Elfrida opened her mouth to start arguing, 'well now you're back in your Own Time and *that's* not right. What *do* you want? Come on. You can't have it both ways!'

'Aren't you being a bit hard on her?' asked Sir Patrick.

Roy shook his head.

'No. I want the truth. Well, Elfrida?'

Roy was pretty angry and he had a right to be so really, as apart from being made a Squire (and he could hardly call himself that at Queensam Comprehensive) he had experienced a fairly trying time with Elfrida one way and another. He had tried to do his best for her, he had dealt with a whole series of problems, he had spent nearly all his money and he had heard his own town being criticised over and over again. Added to which his shoes were hurting like anything.

There was a long, rather embarrassing silence and then a deep, husky voice, a new voice, spoke from the shadows.

'Well, well, well,' it said. 'Come on Elfrida, answer the lad's question. Oh you *are* a troublesome girl. What *am* I going to do about you, eh? But welcome back all the same.'

A smallish, stout man with a round face and a fringe
of grey beard stepped out of the bushes and stabbed
a finger in Elfrida's direction. She backed up against
Woolly who took no notice as he had at long last

found a very tasty bush and was eating its fruits as hard as he could go.

'It's Wickery,' whispered Elfrida.

'Course it's me, you silly stupid, difficult girl. Oh, if you only knew the troubles you've caused. Now listen gentlemen do, I beg you. Here's this girl who works quite well, I grant you, in the kitchens. A nice girl, good character, willing to learn a bit, BUT ... one, she will argue.'

Elfrida pushed her toe into the dust and looked at it intently. Sir Patrick nodded and then quickly stopped himself from doing so.

'Two; she won't stop EATING.'

Elfrida wriggled her other toe and glanced at Roy who somehow just managed to stop himself nodding quite violently.

'So what do I do? What *can* I do?' demanded Old Wickery, 'but put a spell on her. Only trouble was it went a bit wrong. She was meant to sleep just for a little while, and then wake up with a smaller appetite. only me hand slipped while I was putting out the flower petals and ... well ... it could have happened to *anyone*! There she was invisible *and* the castle, and then a breeze came up the river and before I knew what was happening, the petals were going in all directions and, well, to be perfectly fair and truthful with you gentlemen, this particular spell went all over the place. Very nasty it was. Most unpleasant. Trying. It's been a very difficult time one way and another.'

Woolly hiccupped, Sir Patrick leant on his stick-sword and stared at Old Wickery, Elfrida twisted the end of her plait, the See-Through Mr Wickens smiled and nodded in a dreamy sort of way and it was left to Roy to kick off his shoes, wriggle his toes and then stride forwards until he and Old Wickery were face to face although Roy's face was just slightly higher up.

'Trying!' said Roy furiously. 'Difficult! Do you know how much damage you've done? There's poor Sir Patrick here has lost his job, and Woolly is hundreds and hundreds of years out of His Time, while Elfrida's caught between This Time and My Time. *I* haven't got any money left and I'm dreadfully late for my newspaper round and, what's more,' and Roy's voice got angrier and angrier, 'it's just because you're a rotten magician or whatever your job is...'

'Future diviner; writer in sand; illuminator of manuscripts,' whispered Elfrida from behind Woolly.

'Well anyway it's your fault that Queensam's such a boring place in My Time. Yes, now I come to think of it, it's covered in your rotten old invisible magic from one end to the other. It's the reason for all our "keep off" notices and "keep quiet" signs and nobody speaking to anybody or being allowed to have cats and dogs in flats. It's your not-properly-working spells which makes people so bad-tempered and cross with each other. It's not Elfrida's fault, it's *your's* and WHAT ARE YOU GOING TO DO ABOUT IT?'

As Roy spoke, with one finger jabbing at Old Wickery's chest, they had been moving on so that now they had reached open ground and ahead of them was the oblong shaped castle with a turret at each of its four corners. It was quite a small castle, not nearly as big as the Council buildings in Queensam New Town, and it had brambles and bracken growing up against its walls and there was a well about fifty yards from it across the grass, and a path which showed the way to the Roman villa (and beyond which in a few hundred years a formal Elizabethan manor would be built) and some distance further on still the start of a wood which quite soon became a great forest that rolled on and on until it vanished into the mist.

'How beautiful it is,' said Sir Patrick, who hadn't really been listening for some time. 'So peaceful, so calm and tranquil. Oh, I do wish I had lived now ... in Your Time. I could play a lute, and write and learn spells and fight dragons.'

'There aren't any,' said Elfrida. 'Only the bad people in the long boats and He protects us from them.'

'And perhaps I might even meet your General,' said Sir Patrick. 'I've always wanted to. I know I'm not real Knightly material, but ...'

'STOP, STOP, STOP,' shouted Roy. 'Mr Old Wickery, I've got to get back for my paper round because Gran's depending on me. WHAT ARE YOU GOING TO DO ABOUT YOUR SPELL?'

'Whaaaa,' said Woolly helpfully and hiccupped violently and then yawned.

'I, I, I,' said Old Wickery wringing his hands. 'Elfrida girl, you are difficult and troublesome and you *won't* learn and you *do* eat too much, but tell me the truth, and I deserve to know it seeing that I've chased after you in my Future and Back into the Past and very tiring its been at that, do you really wish to live in this Queens Elm Town?'

'Yes,' said Elfrida without stopping to think. 'Oh yes, I do. I do!'

'Then we'll have to have a swap,' said Old Wickery. 'I may only have 5 "W Levels" but I do know *that*! Professor Merlin, His Court Magician taught me that particular rule. You have to have a swap. So who'll exchange, eh?'

Roy and Woolly and the see-through-Mr-Wickens gaped at each other and then the voice of Sir Patrick rang out strongly in the clearing.

'I will. Oh yes I will...'

'You'll miss being in the library,' said Roy, 'and your moped.'

'You really are a proper Knight after all,' said Elfrida. The see-through-Mr Wickens opened and shut his mouth but nobody could hear a word he said. Woolly said,

'Waaaaaaaa.'

'Yes indeed,' agreed Sir Patrick stroking him, 'one day I'll know enough to get you back to Your Own Time, but until then we'll look after each other. You'll like that won't you, eh?'

'Waaaaaa.'

'Well, that appears to be settled then,' said Old Wickery, blowing out his grey whiskers with an enormous sigh. 'And a great relief it is too, because the last thousand years has been a *dreadful* strain on me. Sir ... what is your name?'

'Sir Patrick,' said Elfrida quickly.

'Oh,' said Old Wickery, 'Sir Patrick, I'm very pleased to meet you, I'm sure, Sir. I need an assistant. My work is expanding so rapidly because spells become more and more complicated. Tell me, can you read?'

'Yes, *and* write,' said Sir Patrick, 'and I can count and subtract and cast a few simple spells and fight and see into the future—and play the lute-guitar extremely loudly—and tell stories and rescue Princesses and...'

'Enough,' interrupted Old Wickery, 'you are a most talented young man and you are *exactly* what we need in these troublesome times. He and Merlin will be delighted to meet you and...'

'Are you sure,' said Roy, gripping hold of Mr Patrick's wrist, 'that you really want to stay here? It won't be the same you know.'

'Yes, I am sure. This is My Time,' replied the ex-children's librarian of Queensam New Town. 'I've never been as sure of anything before. I belong here. People can get born out of their right Times you know. I was one of them, and I never *felt* right until now. And I've got no family to worry about me. And you're all the friends I've ever had. O.K.?'

They all shook hands and if Elfrida and Woolly sniffed a bit everybody else looked somewhere else and the last glimpse they had was of Mr, that is, Sir Patrick, down on one knee with his crash helmet under his arm and Woolly yawning alongside him and Old Wickery throwing white petals into the air and smiling from ear to ear with relief and then at the very, very last second, Roy caught a glimpse of a group of horsemen appearing out of the forest, talking and smiling in the hazy sunlight. Their leader was a broad-shouldered man with a smiling, strong sort of face. He glanced towards the castle, and then cantered forwards with his hand held out towards Sir Patrick who'd gone as red as an apple. It was the kind of face that makes you know at once who it belongs to and Roy heard himself saying.

'That's him! That's King Arthur! Oh flip! Oh goodness—that's *him* ...'

And then Old Wickery's spell took over and everything turned upside down and there was a great rushing sound. And at the same moment Elfrida's hand slid out of Roy's and when he shouted her name Old Wickery called back, 'Don't fret boy—she'll be back in Your Time as soon as my assistant and I have worked out the right spells.'

'Roy ...' said Elfrida faintly and then she was gone.

'And about time too,' said the voice of Granny Hatch, 'where *have* you been Roy? Oh and you've lost your shoes! I've been waiting and waiting, thinking you were going to be late and suddenly everything got so noisy. I don't know what's happening all of a sudden. Look you!'

And she was quite right, for a great buzz of talk was rising up all over Queensam and people were coming out of their front doors and walking down their garden paths and leaning on their garden gates and talking to each other. In fact they were chattering away as though their lives depended on it. And Councillor Wickens, who felt as though he had just recovered from some kind of bad tempered illness, was for the first time in his life smiling from ear-lobe to ear-lobe as he drove his milk-float down Oak Crescent and then, with a chuckle, straight across Keep Off Park, singing at the top of his voice as he did so.

The Mayor, Mr Williams, on an impulse telephoned a great number of people with the ultimate result that the new buildings which had been under construction (the very same that Woolly had been tethered to) were redesigned as an Entertainments Centre for everybody, which in the end meant that no more vandals attacked the Town Hall as they were too busy having a good time playing games, taking part in competitions and generally making a great deal of noise and fuss and thoroughly enjoying themselves.

So that through the long warm autumn day and night the spell that had lain over Queensam for so long vanished slowly and at the same time other magic forces came into being as Sir Patrick and Old Wickery worked and worked in Their Own Time.

And the next day, which happened to be the last day of the holidays, Roy, who felt very odd somehow, went to deliver all the usual papers and when he saw Mr Forester of Oak Drive and Mr Forester said,

'My word Roy, you *have* grown...'

Roy only said 'yes', and then pedalled on until at the very end of his paper round he came to Mr Cliff's house. Mr Cliff and Bouncer were waiting for him and both of them were smiling and smiling underneath their white moustaches.

'Morning Roy,' said Mr Cliff. 'The most extraordinary thing has happened. Remember me telling you about our niece, Ann, who died out in Canada? Well she left us a great-niece! And what's more she's come to live with us. Isn't that marvellous? Hm?'

And out of the front door came a girl with a freckled face and long hair and a very wide smile.

'Her name,' said Mr Cliff, putting his arm round his great-niece's shoulder, 'is Elfrida. Her Aunty and I call her Elfie for short. Elfie, this is Roy Hatch.'

Roy and Elfrida shook hands without saying a word and then Roy clambered back on to his bike, as Mr Cliff said fondly,

'And she's got the biggest appetite in the whole of Queensam, I'll be bound. Come on Elfie, back to breakfast.'

'I'll bet she has,' said Roy, standing on the pedals of his bike, 'good old Elfrida OUCH! ! ! !'

'There,' said Granny Hatch, who had been waiting for him, 'I knew you'd hit your head on that lintel. I knew it only you wouldn't listen. You never do.'

Granny Hatch's voice went on and on up and down

while Roy gulped down his breakfast. Tomorrow he would be back at school and this quite astonishing holiday would be finished. A holiday full of all kinds of unusual things such as escaped Princesses and prehistoric animals and The Cross Lady and a dog who was partly invisible, and a Children's Librarian who became a Knight of old and...

'Ouch!' said Roy for the second time.

'There you are then,' said Granny Hatch, 'you won't listen to me. Nobody can tell you anything, but if you will keep on hitting your head it can only mean one thing. You've grown. Did I tell you that Mrs Swift has lost her lodger, gone off into the blue he has...'

'I *can't have*,' said Roy quite forgetting everything else.

'Your jeans don't fit, your shoes don't fit, you keep hitting your head...'

'I have,' said Roy twisting round and looking at the pencil marks on the wall, 'I have, I have, I HAVE...'

And he had. He had grown like anything. Over three inches during the summer holidays.

'YIPEEEEEEEEE,' shouted Roy as he took off on his paper round the following morning, absolutely standing on his pedals and not caring in the least if he zigzagged across the Park as everybody else was doing it too. 'I've grown, I've grown, I've grown... Hi Elfrida, are you home?'

'Now then, now then,' said Mr Wickens, drawing up in his milk float. 'Want to wake up the whole neighbourhood do you? Not that it needed waking up for this last couple of days. Everybody's out and about so early that it takes me twice as long to do my rounds. Still if you can't pass the time of day with a few friends, life isn't worth living, that's what I say.'

'Do you?' said Roy, getting out a copy of the local paper, the headline of which said, 'QUEENSAM AUTUMN FAIR, ALL WELCOME. KEEP PARK OCT 1.' A week ago it would have been impossible to imagine Mr Wickens of all people saying a thing like that.

'Goodness,' said Roy, hitching up his new jeans, 'Old Wickery and Sir Patrick must have been doing *over* time! Perhaps Merlin's been giving them a hand, and even He may have been helping too, I suppose . . .'

Mr Wickens came rattling down the Cliffs' garden path with some empty bottles which he dumped in the back of his float and then, with a rather redder face than usual, he said, 'You know, Roy, just between us, we both know that we haven't been very friendly in the past. I don't know why, but I want things to be different from now on. No, no don't speak for a minute, lad. And don't laugh. But I had a curious sort of dream a short time back, a dream in which I was a boy again and up to all a boy's tricks. That was nice, I enjoyed it. Then it turned nasty, almost like a nightmare. It was like I became almost invisible so that folks could only half see me and they couldn't hear me at all.'

'It must have been very frightening,' said Roy,

leaning on his handlebars as he recalled the See-Through-Mr Wickens who had been yet another victim of Old Wickery's inefficiency.

'It WAS, boy, it WAS. You were there too, *and* that circus animal—there's been no word about that being missing by the way—and funny enough, so was Mr Cliff's niece and,' and Mr Wickens juggled with a cut loaf and some yoghurt cartons, 'and that young librarian chap who's done a bunk. I'd been feeling a bit bad about him, but in this dream I'm telling you of, he'd become a Knight like in the Olden Days and he was as contented as could be.'

'That's nice,' said Roy, who out of the corner of his eye had seen Elfrida slipping quietly down the garden path to listen. She was wearing a T-shirt and jeans and she'd washed her hair.

'Yes, it was, but the funniest bit's yet to come. There was an old chap in this dream. Fat, red face, bit of a strange sort of a beard and do you know, Roy, it was like seeing myself in a mirror. Only I haven't got a beard, of course. Grumpy, complaining sort of chap he was too and all of a sudden I thought, "my goodness" I thought, "is that what I'm really like" and I woke up all of a sudden. And do you know what, I'd dozed off sitting in my car parked near the Motorway. Dozed clean off. Funny, wasn't it?'

'Very,' said Roy and Elfrida together and Elfrida added,

'And how do you feel now, Mr Milkman?'

'Oh fine,' said Mr Wickens, 'never felt better in

me life. The truth is, just between us three, it's like
as if a cloud's sort of rolled away and the sun's shin-
ing nice and bright. 'Morning to you. And it's our
secret, all of what I've told you about my dream
and that, right?'

And Mr Wickens laid one large finger against the
side of his nose and winked and Elfrida and Roy
winked back. The milk float rattled on to the next
house and Bouncer came heaving and panting down
the garden path and gazed up happily at Roy who
scratched him behind one ear as he said,

'I still don't understand *everything*. Like the cave,
and what's happened to Mr, I mean Sir Patrick's
moped, and anyway will he be all right and what
about you and ... ?'

'Don't,' said Elfrida, 'don't, don't, don't ask questions. It's all come out right in the end and everybody
is going to live happily ever after, just like in the
stories that the Head Scullery Maid used to tell us
after candles-out. You'll see.'

'Want to have a ride of my bike?' Roy asked.

Elfrida hesitated.

Neither Roy nor Elfrida, neither Bouncer nor Mr
Wickens, who was now whistling as he delivered milk
further down the road, noticed that the mist was
peeling away from Queensam New Town so that
with every passing second the invisible magic which
for so long had lain over the whole area, was fading
away never to return.

'I won't have a ride on your bi-cycle at the moment,'
Elfrida said carefully, 'because ...'

'I know,' said Roy starting to laugh, which made Bouncer start going woof woof woof in a coughing sort of way, 'I know you're...'

'HUNGRY!' said Elfrida-the-scullery-Maid-Princess. 'See you later.'

'See you later,' said Roy and off he went down the street, passing Mr Wickens' float and when he had got up enough speed Roy got one foot on the saddle, and the other up in the air in his flying eagle act and, just for a fleeting second, he glanced sideways at Keep Park. But there was nothing to be seen at all, except for people exercising their dogs, or walking briskly or talking.

'And everybody really did live happily ever after,' said Roy and began to work on a new balancing trick which took him all the way home to The Corner Stores where Granny Hatch was just dishing up his breakfast.

It was bacon, Marmite, fried bread *and* a sausage.

ENID BLYTON is Dragon's bestselling author. Her books have sold millions of copies throughout the world and have delighted children of many nations. Here is a list of her books available in Dragon Books:

FIRST TERM AT MALORY TOWERS	50p	☐
SECOND TERM AT MALORY TOWERS	50p	☐
THIRD YEAR AT MALORY TOWERS	50p	☐
UPPER FOURTH AT MALORY TOWERS	50p	☐
IN THE FIFTH AT MALORY TOWERS	50p	☐
LAST TERM AT MALORY TOWERS	50p	☐
MALORY TOWERS GIFT SET	£2·55	☐
6 Books by Enid Blyton		
THE TWINS AT ST CLARE'S	50p	☐
SUMMER TERM AT ST CLARE'S	50p	☐
SECOND FORM AT ST CLARE'S	50p	☐
CLAUDINE AT ST CLARE'S	50p	☐
FIFTH FORMERS AT ST CLARE'S	50p	☐
THE O'SULLIVAN TWINS	50p	☐
ST CLARE'S GIFT SET	£2·55	☐
5 Books by Enid Blyton		
MYSTERY OF THE BANSHEE TOWERS	50p	☐
MYSTERY OF THE BURNT COTTAGE	50p	☐
MYSTERY OF THE DISAPPEARING CAT	40p	☐
MYSTERY OF THE HIDDEN HOUSE	50p	☐
MYSTERY OF HOLLY LANE	50p	☐

All these books are available at your local bookshop or newsagent, or can be ordered direct from the publisher. Just tick the titles you want and fill in the form below.

Name ....

Address ....

....

Write to Dragon Cash Sales, PO Box 11, Falmouth, Cornwall TR10 9EN

Please enclose remittance to the value of the cover price plus:

UK: 18p for the first book plus 8p per copy for each additional book ordered to a maximum charge of 66p

BFPO and EIRE: 18p for the first book plus 8p per copy for the next 6 books, thereafter 3p per book

OVERSEAS: 20p for first book and 10p for each additional book

Granada Publishing reserve the right to show new retail prices on covers, which may differ from those previously advertised in the text or elsewhere.